CEFERINO

One of a kind.

Ricardo Alves-Ferreira

To My Mother Concepcion, for her stories and encouragement to learn.

Ramon series, book three

Ceferino.

Part one.

In the truth of your love
I shall find the path to your heart,
We shall build a better world
Young and unafraid today, tomorrow we shall lead the way.

Brava had a long flight back; she used her time to daydream about the wedding, her family and friends being at La Cintura. Thirty six hours later she finally arrived at Puerto. Cooper was eagerly waiting for her to make her way through the gates. As she walked out the gates he ran to hug her; they embraced in a long hug, just holding each other close to take in their presence. Cooper kissed her, caressed her face and told her how much he missed her. Brava shed some tears and told him she missed him terribly also. She asked about Gato, and how things had run whilst she was away. Cooper said that everything was good, things had run smoothly and there were twenty one volunteers at the camp. He asked about her speech and the response of the people to her talks and presentation. Brava told him how well received she was and how much interest she had aroused with the students.

Cooper asked if she had thought about what he had proposed. Brava smiled and kissed him again. "Yes, yes I'll marry you".

Cooper was ecstatic; he jumped in the air and screamed to all who could hear. "I'm getting married!!!" the people in the streets turned around to see who was shouting, and whistle with the understanding of what was happening. Brava and Cooper embraced once more.

Brava told Cooper that her whole family would come to the wedding; Ramon would fly back with Saraphina, her nephew Atticus and her niece Violet. The kids were lovely and would enjoy sometime in the jungle. They were eager to meet Gato and see the wild life of the forest.

Cooper asked how soon they would be coming, had she thought of a date.

Brava responded that she had given them a month, "I think that we should marry on the first of April. I know its April fool's day but I like the idea that it's called the day of the innocent in Spanish. It would make it the more special because I think that innocence is important in love. It means that our love is not corrupted by selfish reasons and that we are in the magic of it."

Cooper kissed her again and with tears in his eyes said, "I told you, you've changed my world and I want to live with you in it for the rest of my life."

Brava was happy, she loved him and Cooper loved her. She had seen the world out there and was happy to be home, she had made the jungle her home, there was purpose in her life and now she was about to start her married life to become the mother of the future. To educate and nurture a new kind of species, the human being of the future; the Kings and Queens that will carry forward her work, her beliefs and the new way of thinking about how we live on this earth. She was going to lead by example, as she had mentioned at her presentation at Deakin University; "We are the mothers of the future, the first educators of a nation. We are the gate way for the Kings and Queens of the future. We can nurture men that will be sensitive and balanced; and will embrace the human family with all their differences to live productively and conscious of our actions and their impact on the planet"

Ramon spent the month of March doing healing workshops with people that had heard of his shamanic understandings. They wanted to learn how to be a better healing channel; it was mostly the understanding of themselves that they sought as an end result. "People have great ideas, great expectations. However they don't realise that one must walk the walk talk and talk. The life of a shaman or a healer is a way of life and not something you do part-time." he would say as he opened the healing workshops.

Saraphina continued working with Ramon on the understanding and assimilation of her past lives memories. They meditated about the power of the jaguar tooth necklace she had kept for years and never understood. Ramon told her; she could use it to aid her development and find her feet as a channel. Over the weeks that passed she began to understand that most of the memories from past lives were related to a greater knowing; one that she had to come to terms with; for it revealed deeper meaning and when put into perspective gave her powers beyond the capabilities of the ordinary human being. Her memories related to coming to terms with a journey with Mykah, they had been together many times before; somehow things never did work out for them. The lessons she had to learn were beyond the physical body and a life on earth.

Ramon explained that Putuma would be instrumental in a deeper cleansing of her mind and body. The Ayahuasca ceremony would give her eyes to see what she needed to understand and answers to her questions, however it would also be an experience that she may find excruciating. Saraphina had asked Mykah for time out; she needed to do things for herself and would return to him with clear mind and heart. Mykah had kissed her and responded that whatever she needed was fine with him. He would wait for her return from South America and was anticipating the time when they could be together without any fears.

It was so that the month passed them by and arrangements to fly to Peru were made and ready. The children were excited and Saraphina was uncertain about so many things. However she found it within herself to keep it all together and take the steps necessary to make things right for all of them. Ramon was aware that she had reservations and kept a close watch on her. He entertained the children through the flight with stories about monkeys, and ant eaters, jaguars and mythological stories of ancient times. Finally and after many hours of flying and flight connections they arrived in Puerto ready to enjoy and participate in Brava's wedding.

Marita had prepared the best food she could make; local products never tasted by guests from overseas were waiting. Fruits only found in the forest had been juiced, and others sliced on trays; flowers had been arranged to decorate the bridal table. Marita was happy to see Ramon, she knew he'd be arriving in the next hour or so and she couldn't contain her excitement, they had become good friends and she had learned to admire him.

Brava was being assisted by two volunteers, the girls had done her hair in a range of ways; they had plaited fine plaits in groups of a dozen and entwined white flowers through them. The veil hung weightlessly from her hair almost like a butterfly had landed to rest upon her. The long flowing skirt was ankle length exposing her bare feet, hugging her hips snug around her waist. The bodice was matching white lace tightly fitted to her upper body, sleeves that fell off the shoulder like a strand of white lace in flower patterns. Brava was the picture of youth, the embodiment of life and the future; the maiden about to become the woman. She was at the moment when human beings trade their childhood for adulthood and begin a journey of exploration, union and sharing.

Cooper was ready also; he wore his best jungle clothes, his khaki short pants, and a new white shirt loose at the sleeves, and brown sandals. His hair combed for the first time in months and slight stubble of a beard well-trimmed. His eyes were green as the forest, and they showed love and commitment, there was no trace of fear to be found.

As the time for the ceremony was approaching the sound of motors was heard down river. Marita ran to the river bank to wait for the guests that were finally arriving. Ramon waved at Marita and she jumped up and down with excitement clapping her hands like a child about to get ice cream. The rest of the passengers sat still holding on to the boat rails with fear. Marita spotted the woman that wore a large brimmed hat with a net falling from it, as if she was inside a mosquito net. She thought it strange, however she had seen worse before; she laughed to herself and waited to see the display that would unfold.

The boat moored and Ramon jumped out to embrace Marita with a giggle of old friends. He hugged her and she held him tight; they were fond of each other and had grown to understand their ways. Ramon turned around and pointing at the people in the boat, he said; "Mi familia" "My family".

Marita smiled and welcome them all. Saraphina was the last one to stand up, she had been holding on to the boat with a grip that she could not undo. Her stomach was turned upside down after the boat ride and she didn't feel stable on her feet. Ramon encouraged her to stand up; the mosquito net that hanged from her hat was the length of her body. Marita laughed out loud unable to stop herself at such sight. Ramon looked at her and shrugged his shoulders.

Saraphina oblivious to what was happening tried to make it across the length of the boat. The boat driver smiled at her predicament thinking in his head that she would fall into the water. She took a step up and jumped of the boat to the river bank, as she took the second step she tripped on the net that she wore and fell flat on her face. Marita laughed even louder and so did everybody there; the children thought it was the funniest thing they had ever seen. Ramon helped her up and looked at her with a question in his eyes. Saraphina stood up and took her hat off saying, " Fine, I know it's ridiculous, but if those bot fly's bite me you'll be in so much trouble and I'll run away, I'll even swim down river." She abruptly took the hat off her head and wriggled her way out of the net. People laughed again as the vision was too funny not to laugh. Ramon smiled and said "There, much better now, Yes?"

The group made their way to the camp and took place among the other guests, the children could not contain their amazement at seeing the birds that flew by and the monkeys jumping from branch to branch in the tree canopies. The heat was humid and heavy; the sun was beginning to gain strength at its midday point.

Brava stepped out of her hut, looking immaculate with a smile that enchanted everyone present and made Ramon and Saraphina well up with tears in their eyes. The Bride and Groom were ready to make their vows; the medicine woman from the Asheninca tribe was the celebrant. She had incense and feathers, she used these items to smudge and fan the couple symbolising a cleansing from any negative energies. Afterwards as the couple recited their vows with each promise she placed a ribbon, four colours were used representing the four cardinal points.

The medicine woman asked, "Brava is you ready to take this man in marriage?"

Brava, "Yes I am"

"Cooper are you ready to take this woman in marriage?"

Cooper, "Yes I am"

"In the presence of all guests gathered here today, their witnessing shall be a sign of legal commitment in marriage for these two lovers who today unite in marriage; to start a life of adulthood and join the community as husband and wife. Brava recite your first promise".

Brava, "I promise to see and welcome each day as the sun rises as a new beginning in our life, giving us opportunity to join our strength and work side by side."

Cooper, "I promise to see each day as an opportunity to share my strength, my commitment to you and work side by side."

The medicine woman placed a yellow ribbon over their hands, signifying a new beginning, a new day and the sunrise.

Brava, " I promise to be conscious each day as I lay to rest beside you of my actions toward you and rectify any hurt that I may have caused you involuntarily."

Cooper, "I promise to review my day each night as I lay to rest beside you and find that I have included you in my actions and plans of that day."

The medicine woman placed a red ribbon over their hands, representing the sun set, the night and the wisdom of experience.

Brava, "I promise to include you in my future plans, in sickness and in health, throughout all our days, and respect you for who you are today."

Cooper, "I promise to care today and the rest of our days, hoping to learn from the wisdom of life to be your guardian and your mate"

The medicine woman placed a white ribbon over their hands representing wisdom, healing and new beginnings.

Brava, "I promise to forgive any mistakes you make in the light of unconscious thought and without malice and move from past errors to the present time."

Cooper, "I promise to forgive any unconscious shortfalls in consideration from your part regarding my inclusion, without holding grudges and release the past to look and learn together for our future."

The medicine woman placed a black ribbon over their hands representing south, the past and release. Following the last promise she tied all ribbons together in a knot binding their promise to each other.

Gato walked slowly down the aisle made by the guests, with a white ribbon around his neck that held the two rings for the couple. Cooper pulled one of the ribbon ends and untied the rings from Gato's neck; then placed one on Brava's finger with one final promise.

"May this ring be a symbol of my love and commitment to you Brava, our life and future together till the earth calls our name." Cooper slid the ring on to Brava's finger.

Brava took the other ring and placed it on Cooper's finger.

"May this ring be the symbol of our union, our choice and commitment to one another, instilling respect and honour for each other till Mother Earth calls our name." Brava slid the ring into Cooper's finger.

The ribbons were placed around the cover of a book that guests would sign with greetings and good wishes; for the couple to keep as a reminder of their union. The medicine woman chanted a song and smudged the couple with a burning stick of sage and mint, fanning the smoke over them as blessing and cleansing for their new beginning. Marita made a call in the form of a bird sound and asked all the guests to take part in the food laid out in the dining area. Everybody congratulated the newlyweds and took photos of the couple. Ramon was proud and hugged the young couple contented that they would be strong together. He shook Cooper's hand and looking into his eyes said; "I know you are aware of who Brava is as a woman and an individual, if you respect her always for who she is you'll be a man who will enjoy the fruits of marriage as it should be."

Saraphina and the kids where around Brava; Saraphina cried as she hugged her little sister. Violet told Brava how beautiful she looked and how much she loved the environment around them. "This place is so fun!"

Atticus gave Brava a hug and smiled, he wanted to pat the cat more than anything else. Brava called out for Gato to come over, telling Atticus he could pat the cat as much as he wanted. Atticus eyes lit up with glee.

Putuma made his way to Ramon and Brava, he offered Brava and Cooper a blanket woven by the weavers of his tribe as a wedding gift. The blanket showed patterns and flowers of a sacred nature, familiar to the newlyweds. Brava was thankful and kissed him in return. Ramon introduced Putuma to Saraphina, stating that he was the shaman willing to take Saraphina through the Ayahuasca ceremony. Saraphina smiled shyly and responded that she was terrified at the thought. Putuma assured her that she would be safe and he would make sure she was not afraid when the time came to perform the ceremony.

Ramon had noticed a man standing at the edge of the gathering, his appearance was native but not of the region. He asked Marita who the man was and Marita surprised for forgetting to introduce them said, "He is a Mapuche Indian from the south of Argentina, his name is Jabaro, he arrived two days ago to speak to you, he has been waiting to meet you."

They walked over to the man and Marita introduced them to each other. The Mapuche Indian asked Ramon to take a walk with him along the river bank. As they walked along the path leading to the river Jabaro, the Mapuche Indian; told Ramon that he was there to ask Ramon to follow him south to Argentina, the Patagonian people had heard of the Shaman who had helped the Arhuaco and the Mamo and now the Kakataivo and the other local tribes. His people had been trying to stand up for their rights and had been suffering for one hundred and fifty years of turmoil in their land; the authorities of Chile and Argentina had disregarded their native rights and were pushing them into extinction

"Ramon I cannot go back home without you coming with me. Would you please help us?"

Ramon looked at the crowd of people gathered around Brava and Cooper; he looked over at Saraphina and the kids. He felt the medallion glow in his chest and a rustle of leaves sang over him. The voice of Don Ignacio said in his ear; "Are you ready for more adventure?"

Part two.

In the depth of your heart
You will hear my call,
Like an echo or song,
Calling you to the south.

Ramon had left the Mapuche at the table with all the other guests; he walked alone along the river bank, thinking what to do next. Jabaro had stated clearly that he would not return to Argentina without him. Ramon thought of Brava, Saraphina and the kids. They had planned to spend time together and learn about the jungle way of life. The children were excited about the experience. Saraphina needed to relax, cleanse and prepare for the Ayahuasca Ceremony with Putuma. Ramon wanted to be there to guide her with Putuma, she had many demons haunting her and Putuma even though an experienced shaman, would probably benefit from his help. Ramon knew that Saraphina would feel much more trusting if he was there, and it was imperative that she did it the right way.

Ramon sat under a tree, he closed his eyes and meditated about what was expected of him. He felt the medallion glow as his thought evocated Don Ignacio's name; in his mind's eye he saw the familiar figure begin to take form in the distance as the figure approached Don Ignacio's face lit up with the usual warm smile.

"What seems to be troubling you Ramon?" he asked.

"Don Ignacio, my teacher; thank you for being present. I find myself in a predicament. I want to help my daughter Saraphina through her experience of the Ayahuasca so she can deal with the memories that have been unleashed in her mind. She needs to understand and close the fear she experiences every time a new memory presents itself to her. Jabaro wants me to follow to his land and help his people with their issues and I don't know how long I can detain him here. He already has been waiting for me for over a week and I don't know if I will be of any real help to them." Ramon expressed concern.

"There are missions in your life Ramon, as there were missions in mine. A shaman must trust that when he is called. He is called, not to do things out of his own power that would expand his energy and deplete him eventually; not being able to receive messages clearly, because his mind is not listening to the voice of spirit. His mind would be doing what he thinks is right. You are an instrument, the Great Spirit will bring people to you every time it requires you to be the physical presence, his representative, and he works through you. Ramon you must trust the Great Spirit and its plan. If Jabaro is here requiring you to follow him to his land, you must act accordingly. Perhaps Jabaro would be able to spend a few days here with you all and see the work of the Great Spirit through you first hand. Ask and you shall be granted, the universe always has more time; for time is but a construct of mankind." Don Ignacio's voice was silent for a moment.

"I'm sorry Don Ignacio, it isn't that I don't trust the voice of spirit, it's just perhaps that I feel that the world is chasing me and wanting me to fix things, when I'm only a simple man that finds it all too big. The honour of being an instrument for the Great Spirit's work humbles me and I confess the mortal man in me gets afraid of not being capable of dealing with the required effort from my part." Ramon spoke in a low voice reflecting his humbleness.

"The Great Spirit never gives us anything we can't handle. And without telling you too much you are in for a great discovery, it will take you back to your childhood and it will bring memories you have forgotten. Ramon, remember that we have been with you all your life, we know what you can do. We are with you and shall give you access to all you need for the completion of your task. I walk with you every step. I know we shall speak again soon, and I shall be there to guide you through understanding. Go speak to Jabaro and buy time so that you can be with your family and make them feel safe." Don Ignacio landed a hand on Ramon's shoulder as he always used to do when walking together along the Black Line in Colombia.

"I would like to thank you for looking after my girls through their entire lives. Brava is an amazing young woman and she has learned to use the jaguar tooth necklace very well with expert skill. Saraphina is learning and it was a great surprise to know that you had been with her all along as well! We were all so excited to learn that we are part of a spiritual family that goes back eons in time on the earth plan and that our work has always been to assist mankind along their path. Thank you once again Don Ignacio." Ramon smiled at his teacher, the old man smiled back with the tenderness that made him cry every time. The old man was the embodiment of love and wisdom. Ramon felt his heart melt every time they spoke.

Don Ignacio's form dissipated into the ether and Ramon was again alone listening to the sounds of the birds and monkey's. The river current made a gurgling sound and the breeze rustled the leaves above him like wind chimes. Ramon saw Jabaro standing not far from him; the man had followed Ramon and stood silently waiting for Ramon to finish his meditation. Jabaro wanted confirmation from Ramon that he was able to assist and would go to Patagonia with him. Ramon waved a hand at him asking for Jabaro to join him a while. Ramon put a question to Jabaro about how long he could remain with them before departing for Patagonia.

"Jabaro", said Ramon. "I need to assist my daughter with some healing work, Putuma and I are taking Saraphina through the Ayahuasca Ceremony, she needs cleansing and understanding on some issues she has been experiencing, these issues are affecting her life and I need to be here for her. Could I ask that you remain with us for two weeks before we go to your land and your people?"

Jabaro, smiled and his shoulders dropped, a sign of satisfaction obvious to Ramon. Then he said, "I will wait as long as you need me to wait Ramon. I'm very happy you have accepted our request to visit our land and help us stand strong to face the changes that are coming." Jabaro smiled and his eyes filled with tears of joy; his mission to bring Ramon with him to Patagonia was about to be achieved and he felt proud of accomplishing his task.

Over the next few days Brava and Cooper worked on the camp's construction needs, the amount of interest from volunteers had increased three fold since Brava had travelled overseas and given speeches at the Australian Universities. The United States students had also caught on and the number of applications demanded more huts to be constructed. The children participated in the construction process; learning the technique of weaving palm tree leaves through the uprights that made the walls. Atticus was in his element, he was enjoying the freedom of the jungle, the animal species and following monkeys along the transects with Cooper every morning. Violet had become very interested in the art work of the Shipibo tribe and she learnt the method of painting geometric patterns inspired by flowers. The Shipibo women were kind to her; they loved her platinum hair and every time she brushed it they would ask for the strands caught in the brush. Violet gave it to them, she knew that there was magic in her hair, or at least she knew that the Shipibo women felt it as such a token. The women had made sewing strands with her hair and used it to make decorative stitching around their garments. Violets hair shone like gold, and it was long and strong making it easy to thread through a needle. The women made patterns on their clothing and embroidered flowers of gold on the garments lapels. The children were happy and did not seem to be too bothered by the insects. Atticus would return every day with a new bug, large bird eating spiders or snakes he learned to catch with Cooper. He was fascinated by the variety of life forms that the jungle had to offer. The native children liked him, not only because he seemed to speak incessantly but because he had green eyes and blond hair and seemed to be unafraid of anything they showed him. Ramon took it all in, enjoying the interaction that had developed among the tribe's people and the children. He particularly enjoyed the way the children had accepted the ways of the jungle. They didn't seem to mind the lack of electricity and internet. They were busy from dawn to dusk and the variety of activities had many things to offer the curious mind of a child. Gato and Ramon walked along the river bank checking for poachers; it was a way for Ramon to spend time alone with Gato. They had become very close and the cat liked talking to Ramon. He particularly enjoyed the way nature spirits presented themselves to Ramon to teach him of important things like how to extract medicinal juices from trees, leaves and roots. Gato sat next to Ramon and listened, every so often he would offer words of advice however he mainly concerned himself with scanning the river for boats or movement in the water's edge. Ramon talked to Gato about his impending trip and made sure the cat would take care of the people he loved. Gato had responded by saying that he loved them too much to allow anything to happen to them and that he too will miss Ramon while he was away. Ramon patted Gato and spent some time in silence

Saraphina was having a harder time adjusting to the rudimentary set up of the camp. She felt too hot all the time and the sweat dripped constantly from her body. She was encouraged to drink plenty of water as this would begin to assist with her detox and cleanse her body of toxins. She was allowed to smoke, however she had to reduce the number of smokes by three every day. Over a week she had come down to two cigarettes per day. Putuma had been providing meditation sessions with her, and hours of conversation to exercise the emotional need to let it all come out. He wanted her to be ready for the ceremony and the more she let things out of her system the better the experience she would have.

The Ashaninca medicine woman had given Saraphina a healing with vapour treatment and a herbal reading to assist in purifying her mind, body and spirit. Saraphina had enjoyed the healing, even though new to her, it wasn't very invasive and she felt the effects immediately. The medicine woman told her that the smoking was reducing her lung capacity and that it disturbed her sleep patterns. "Too much of it is not good for anybody" she said, "You must learn to respect your body as a temple for the spirit. In temples we burn incense and make offering of smoke, a small amount is ok, too much of it will burn your temple down to the ground", said the woman in a stern voice. Saraphina couldn't help but laugh as the illustration the medicine woman used gave her funny visuals in her mind and she saw herself burning down covered in cigarettes. It was obvious her mind was craving more tobacco and less cleansing.

Saraphina worked with Putuma on dream work. He explained the meaning of dreams and the messages they conveyed. He taught Saraphina how to understand the language of dreams so she could begin to hear the warning, advice or prophesy each dream brought as a gift to her. Saraphina liked the way Putuma addressed every question, explained each session and was ever so patient with her peculiarities. Putuma was a good friend of Ramon and he had taken care of the girl well, getting her ready for the cleansing. He had told him that she was ready to start the cleansing for the Ayahuasca ceremony. He believed that Saraphina was ready. Ramon agreed that the time was right, it had been over a week and she had sweated and changed body mass with the new diet and heat. Consuming great amounts of water had helped purify her system and the hours of meditation guided by Putuma had settled down the stress she had carried within her.

Putuma made preparation for the ceremony at the Kakataivo camp. He believed it was better to do it away from the other volunteers, Saraphina would need privacy and it was best the children didn't see her during the days of ceremony. Ramon helped him build the hut that would house the ritual and helped with the collection of grasses that would cover the floor; and herbal medicines to be used as teas and potions. Saraphina was beginning to anticipate the moment she would be taken into the forest for the cleansing ceremony; however she felt comfortable with the idea that Ramon and Putuma would be the only ones with her. She could not imagine what was going to come out of her memory bank and it was better that she was alone with the men and no one else. These men knew much about her and they had her best interests at heart.

Jabaro entertained himself with the company of Marita, she had made sure he was busy and kept her company. Marita designated tasks for him to do and they worked together in the preparation of the camp's meals. She had a great sense of humour and their laughter was a happy sound heard through the forest. Marita was enjoying the great activities of the camp, the new visitors, guests and volunteers were an amazing mix of people that shared and brought great ideas and stories to the table at meal times. Marita had never been happier and felt fulfilled with the life she was now living at La Cintura. Ramon had been so kind as to bring her a gorgeous silk shawl from overseas. It had colourful butterfly's embroidered on it and it was so large that she wore it as a dress wrapped around her body allowing the air to cool her down from below. She felt beautiful when she wore it and that night she planned to wear it for Jabaro, she was beginning to like him.

Volunteers enjoyed the variety of people from all over the world with amazing stories to tell, every night around the table after dinner there were stories told by Putuma, Ramon or Jabaro and some told by the volunteers themselves. The multicultural blend of stories was a dream come true for some, while others felt afraid of them by taking their meaning literally.

One such story was told by Putuma about their ancient beliefs and how their world was saved from the darkness that prevailed upon earth long ago. He said that his people had recounted the story passed on from generation to generation; he himself had heard it from his grandfather.

"Long before there were others, when only the people of each tribe lived on the earth as the only inhabitants, long before the Incas appeared and ruled, or were even heard of in these kingdoms, our people speak of another being much greater than all others. They affirm that they went for a long time without seeing the sun and that, suffering tremendously with the deficiency of light, they raised great prayers to the revered Gods, asking them to restore the light they lacked; in this manner, there arose from the centre of Lake Titicaca, an island, called the island of the Sun. The sun shining brilliantly, made them very happy. They say that from the land of the noon sun right above them, there came and appeared to them a man of large build whose aspect and persona showed great authority. This man had such supreme power that he levelled the mountains and rose up the plains into large hills, making water flow from rocks. Recognising his supreme power, they called him the creator of all things, father of the sun. He did many great things, because he gave life to men and animals, and from his hand, they received great benefits. According to my grandfather who told it to me, who heard it from his father, who also heard it in the songs they preserved from long ago; this man went towards the north, working many miracles in his journey. They never saw him again. In many places they say that he gave instructions to the men about how to live productively, and that he spoke with love and humility, encouraging them to be good and not cause harm or injury to one another, to love each other and have charity. Most people call him Ticiviracocha, even though he goes by many names, they call him Tuapaca, and in other places he is known as Arnauan or Viracocha. Many temples were built in his name in different places, where they erected stone statues in his likeness. There are large stone figures in the city of Tiahuanaco, meant to represent him and date from that era. They say nothing else about him, nor did he ever return to any part of the jungle.

All the native Indians agree that they were created by this Ticiviracocha or Viracocha, who they believe was a white man, clothed in a white robe around his body, and that he carried a staff and something resembling a book in his hands. After this, they tell a strange story; that after Ticiviracocha created all the people, he came walking to a place where a large group had gathered; Ticiviracocha doing the works of piety and instructing the people he had created on how to live in harmony and productively, announced he wished to leave the land of Peru. He gave a speech to those present, advising them of things which were to happen in the future. He warned them that people shall arrive saying that they were the Ticiviracocha, their God and all creator, and that the people should not believe these impostors. He said that in the coming ages he would send his messengers to teach and support the people of Peru. Having said this, he and his companions went into the ocean and walked away over the waters, without sinking, as if they had been walking on land." Putuma looked at Ramon, a light in his eyes suggesting that Ticivicocha had sent him to help and look after the people of the rain forest.

Volunteers and guests went to bed filled with legends and questions. What was true about anything? How did these people know about Gods from other parts of the universe? And who was to know the truth of it all? The stars twinkled in the sky, an opening above the river let their light reflect on the river surface as if the Milky Way had aligned itself with the curving of the river bank.

Two days had passed and Putuma was ready for Saraphina's Ayahuasca Ceremony; they had made all preparations and had arranged for the children to be looked after by Marita and Brava. Jabaro stayed with them at the camp while the ceremony was being conducted. Saraphina was now nervous; the day had arrived and she was terrified to face her fears. Putuma spoke to her for a while about relaxing and being able to be strong and not go in to the cleansing with fears in her mind. It was better to face things straight on as they presented themselves, instead of anticipating what may be!

"As we enter the sacred space of the Ayahuasca state, we must be like humble disciples that learn from the teacher. The Ayahuasca plant is the plant of the soul. It knows what we need and will show it to us, so that we can learn and then remove the effects of anything blocking our progress." Spoke Putuma reassuringly.

Saraphina nodded and tried to relax by breathing deeply to fill her lungs with plenty of oxygen so that her mind would relax and be clearer. Ramon had asked her to be comfortably dressed, to bring a change of clothes and towels. Putuma lead them through the forest to the ceremonial place. Soon there were smudging sticks burning, to cleanse Saraphina's body and the space around them. Putuma asked Ramon to light a fire and keep water on the boil as there were many teas to be prepared. The small hut was a collection of four walls made by the same construction system used at the camp, palm leaves woven through uprights and a roof made in the same process, thus giving privacy to the ceremony. The sound of the river was heard in the distance like a beat of watery nature. Ramon held his medallion and asked the spirits of the forest to protect the area while they partook in the ceremony. His medallion glowed and made a sound like that of energy swirling, Saraphinas jaguar tooth necklace also glowed.

Putuma sat cross legged against one of the walls, inviting Ramon to sit next to him and Saraphina to sit in the middle of the small room. Putuma began chanting and speaking to the spirit of the Ayahuasca plant asking for healing and understanding. He asked for the spirit of the plant to be gentle and kind but assertive in its effect and healing properties. The pot containing the Ayahuasca mix prepared the day before was warming the tea up; water was boiling in another pot and the preparation of tea began, this second tea was the one to replenish the dehydration experienced by the vomiting and purging of the Ayahuasca cleansing.

Putuma filled the cup and drank from it first, then passed it to Saraphina to drink. He filled another cup and passed it to Ramon to drink.

"We are going to be with you through it all, we shall see what you see and be with you to help and guide you when necessary. We shall only interfere if we believe you are in danger of not coping, otherwise we shall let the Ayahuasca show you what you need to see. Drink the contents of the cup; we shall begin the chants and wait for the effects to take place." said Putuma to Saraphina.

Ramon closed his eyes and chanted with Putuma; Saraphina closed her eyes and tried not to vomit, the taste of the tea was horrendous. She sipped it slowly, and soon the cup was empty. She could hear the gurgling of the tea progress down her body, she felt the texture of her bowel move and lighten as if she needed to go to the toilet; she breathed deeper and tried to relax.

The chanting by the shamans increased and so did the effect of the tea. A dizzy feeling began in her head and a sensation of tingling up the spine followed. The vibration of the chants increased and so did the spinning sensation of Saraphina's head. She dry reached twice but managed not to vomit. Suddenly she fell backwards unable to stop herself. Lying on the floor she felt her body weight change, she felt lighter than before and almost unaffected by gravity. She wanted to open her eyes to see if she was floating but somehow she was unable to do so. Then she felt something coming toward her, something like a black blob, formless undistinguishable. The shape became larger in form and came toward her as if to blanket her whole body. Saraphina felt fear; she was not familiar with what the blackness represented but as the blanket of shadows engulfed her light took its place and she felt as if she was born into another world. She saw herself floating in a rainbow universe, lines of colour going into infinity. She felt as if she could walk the lines like roads and follow their destination; the air seemed to shine like glitter, specks of gold, purple and blue all twinkled in front of her eyes. She could hear the shaman's voices everywhere; their chanting was all around her even though she could not see them. There was a sudden stop of the chanting voices and with it came the dissolving of her vision. In its place a new panorama took shape and as the definition became clearer to Saraphina's mind she distinguished a vision of herself walking through a pine forests. She was young and carried a bucket in her hand as she walked towards a river bank. The colours of the leaves by the river bank showed it was Autumn, the light shone from a low angle marking late afternoon, she bent to fill the bucket with water and as she turned around to walk back home she froze. In front of her stood a young man, dressed in military clothing looking at her with sad eyes. She dropped the bucket and ran to his arms, embracing him and beginning to cry. Saraphina spoke as if she was living the vision. "Don't go, please don't leave me!" the young man whispered, "You know the King demands my presence in his court, I'll be back shortly, take care of our son." The young man walks off leaving Saraphina alone by the river, she turns to refill the bucket and as she turns she sees a platoon of the Kings soldiers coming toward her. They take her as a prisoner and the soldier in charge reads an accusation made against her about conducting witch craft practices and that she would have to be put on trial by the King and his men. Saraphina screamed and tried to free herself from their grip, calling for her husband to help; knowing he was a soldier of the King. The vision changed into a scene of her body being burned at the stake, her eyes radiating two beams of white light descending on her child. Saraphina screamed loudly at this stage, her screams were horrifying with pain; guttural sounds that carried deep painful memories. Her body wriggled like someone who was feeling the burning flames. She tried to move but felt confined by the rope that kept her prisoner, eventually feeling the flames take the air from her breath. Putuma felt Saraphina going into physical shock and intervened.

"This is a memory your soul is showing you Saraphina, stay strong, breathe deeply and calm down, remove yourself from the vision, step back Saraphina, step back and understand."

Saraphina found it hard to remove herself from the flames, as Putuma persisted in guiding her away from the vison, Ramon spoke.

"Saraphina we are looking at the memories you already know, it is obvious you need to see what it tells, however it is a replay of a past life, remember that you are witnessing what happened then to fix the present time in your life." Saraphina felt herself relax as soon as she heard her Father's voice. She knew Ramon wouldn't let her suffer. As she felt herself move back from the fire the vision changed into the image of a serene place, she was wearing a robe of pale purple and gold trimmings, next to her she sees Mykah holding her hand, dressed in robes of equal detail he asked her if she was sure of what they were about to do. She answered positively assuring him that the world of human form was the perfect place to test their love. She added that when a human baby is born it only remembers his divine origins till the awakening of the ego at age seven.

"It is then that our test begins and our journey to find each other on earth would be the greatest test the Gods would ever allow anyone. The danger of forgetting our origins is frightening, but I know in my heart I shall recognize you Mykah. I want to know that our awareness of who we are is beyond the physical limitations of the human form. We are Gods Mykah, and we are permitted to play in what was created for man. Don't you trust yourself?" she asked.

"I fear not finding you, I fear not being able to see the truth of our love in the human form and not be able to control what the ego wants. Are you sure we should do it?" he repeated pleading Saraphina to think about it.

"Mykah, in our world of Gods and Goddesses we know everything. I want to have an adventure in the world of man, where love is the only drive, where one man and one woman can be everything to one another. I want to forget all we know and reduce ourselves to the music of our hearts, to recognise our song and live as an example of human love and devotion for one another. To see each other through the years, to experience our skin age and our hands wrinkle and see through our eyes the fire that still burns in our hearts; don't you want that Mykah?" she asked again.

Mykah hesitated, and kissed her agreeing that that was all he wanted all along also. The vision changed angle as if Saraphina was looking through the thickness of a wall, she sees Mykah talking to the Goddess of love.

"Can you give me a spell that will make the memory of who I am remain once I enter the human form? He asked her.

The Goddess smiled and whispered, "She didn't come to ask me what you have asked me for! Are you sure you want to break your promise to her and cheat? There are consequences and a price to pay; you are aware of that, are you not?" Asked the Goddess thinking of what she would ask in exchange of him.

"I will pay any price as long as you make me remember who I am, so that I can find her. No other man can have her, only I. I shall kill any man that would seduce her or take her away from me. I cannot risk losing her because she may not remember who I am. Name your price!"

The Goddess thought for a moment and then stated her price. "I want your first child as payment, the one that shall be named Keeper. My price is that you kill your first born and send his soul to me. I shall make him a cherub of love and he shall throw his arrow at human hearts, especially those that look for endless love. His name shall go into eternity as Cupid the Angel of Love and will make every human being poisoned by ego be careful of his arrow."

Mykah felt his heart break, the price she demanded was too much, however his selfish love for Saraphina was much deeper and he could delay the birth of his first born life times if necessary.

"I agree to pay your price; you must never allow anyone to know that I have made a deal with you." He bowed and walked away leaving the Goddess watching him go.

Saraphina gasped at what she heard. She cried hearing Mykah agree to sacrifice their first born in exchange for his memory of a God, she felt betrayed by Mykah's deal with the Goddess of Love. She sobbed uncontrollably. Putuma spoke again, he guided her to move on. To allow the memories to reveal what she had to learn.

"Breathe Saraphina, breathe and watch, remove yourself from the vison, watch, witness, learn."

The vision changed again, this time it moved quickly to a life where she was a Priestess and having sworn to a life of virginity and purity she was kidnaped by armed guards from her temple. She had been taken to the ruler of the kingdom where he had confessed to be in love with her beauty. He demanded she renounced the priesthood and marry him giving him a child. She refused saying that she had offered a life of chastity in exchange for enlightenment. She had learned through penance and meditation of a greater love, that of the higher Spirit. She was beyond human bonding and needed not human union. The ruler enraged by her refusal raped her, destroying the sanctity of her body, her spiritual temple. The vision moved forward to the moment where the birth of a child was going on. Saraphina saw herself scream in pain, her actual body rolled around the hut floor as if pushing the baby out. Her breathing was heavy. Putuma and Ramon observed without interrupting. Saraphina's vision went on. The baby now in the hands of the midwife cried. She felt elation at seeing such frail life. As the baby is placed on her bosom she whispers to him.

"You are so beautiful! You shall be named keeper. For you are worth all the pain in the world."

The vision moves forward and Saraphina sees Mykah in the gardens of the palace. She smiles and walks slowly toward him; Mykah's hand rose in the air holding a knife. She hears keeper whimper and realises what's happening. Mykah's hand falls to stab the child taking his life. Saraphina screams in agony at witnessing what had happened. She runs from him afraid of the monster he is. He tries to cover up what his done and chases after her; Saraphina blinded by her tears loses her footing and falls into the abyss crashing onto the rocks below.

Saraphina crying as she witnessed the vision, hears the laughter of the Goddess of Love. The words left in the nothingness of her mind spoke a truth that made her shiver.

"I shall name him Cupid; he shall become the cherub of love."

Saraphinas body started shaking; she rolled around like a spinning top. Her arms and legs trembling and her breathing laboured. She convulsed and as in something surreal she suddenly stopped shaking and straightened up like a pole. Her body floated above the ground and her clothing swayed in the gentle breeze. Putuma and Ramon looked at each other and began chanting, Putuma sang a sacred song that invoked the spirits of light and the room began to fill with a brilliance that was pure and white. Saraphina's body floated mid-air and she was paralysed in a place between spirit and body. Her mind was being released from the worldly confines of perception and her knowing was becoming fully unleashed. Her eyes opened for a few seconds and beams of light shot through the roof of the hut. Putuma and Ramon chanted, bringing her body down to the ground, gently she began to lower herself until she touched the floor of the hut. Then as if triggered by something beyond anybody's control she projectile vomited across the room; soon followed by diarrhoea, runny black faeces that smelled of dead animals and coffee.

Putuma and Ramon chanted while she purged, they burnt smudging sticks and played a simple heart beat on a drum to give Saraphina a sound to anchor her mind to. Half an hour later the shaman undressed her and washed her body with the remaining tea, then rinsed her and wrapped her body in a cotton blanket, carrying her to a hut for the night. Saraphina slept deeply, exhausted and her dreams for the first time in years were of no consequence. She slept for two days straight, not a sound from her. The shaman had cleaned the ceremonial hut, burnt the mess and discussed what they had seen. Saraphina was now open to the collective mind; she would be able to recall any past life, any moment throughout her incarnation on earth with acute detail. Once discussed and assimilated she would be able to go home and take the reins of her life with the relationship that had brought so much grief over centuries and life times. Ramon had spent time thinking about Mykah and the deal he had made long ago in pursuit of his selfish love for her. He knew that Saraphina would not like what she had learnt about him and he could now see that Mykah had not changed. Looking back Ramon could trace his moves; the mural Ramon was engaged to do, the house built close to where Saraphina lived, and other serious things that he had learned about him from Saraphina herself. Ramon waited for her to awake; her brain would be rewiring itself after such a burst of awareness. Her body would be processing the shock and strain experienced through the Ayahuasca ceremony however he knew that soon he would be able to leave knowing that his girls had what it takes to be strong and make it in life.

Saraphina woke up early in the morning of day three, she was starving and light headed. She had the need to drink and eat like she never felt before. Putuma brought a light selection of fruits and breads harvested and made by the women of his tribe. Saraphina ate with gusto, she couldn't get enough into her mouth. Putuma told her to take it easy, as her body was now clean and all the negative energy that had resided within her body was now out. With a new way of thinking about food she could retain the effects of the cleansing for years. Ramon brought her tea, a combination of herbal plants used by the people of the jungle, wild mint leaves and banana salvia leaves for flavour. Saraphina was left to think for a while; later Ramon came to sit by her, it was time they discussed what had transpired during the ceremony. Ramon suggested they take a walk along the forest to exercise their legs, Saraphina had been lying dormant for almost three days and she needed to pump her circulation and breathe oxygen deep into her lungs.

"So tell me what you remember?" asked Ramon.

"What I remember? I remember everything Dad!!! I will stop, and control my disappointment in him. I need to remember that it happened long ago. Not that it makes it right or unimportant, but it is not this life time. Saying that, I'm going home soon. He will have a mouthful from me. I have two children and after seeing what he is capable of, I don't want anything to do with him. Now I understand why I have such a strong reaction to him. Every time he appears in my life I fear him. Now it all makes sense. I cannot believe he can be so selfish as to sacrifice our child for the want of having me to himself. The love we were meant to have was beyond human bounds, pure, selfless and unconditional. He lied from the beginning, he knew all along who I was, where I was and how to find me. His love is selfish, he ripped my heart apart over and over, lifetime after lifetime. No more!"

Saraphina took a deep breath and continued. "Now I remember and know who I am, he is going to be so sorry he ever betrayed me. I shall make things right between us, he will have what he deserves from me. Pity will be one of those things."

Ramon spoke about the wisdom received through the ceremony, the visions and the learnings. "You must remember that now you have access to see within every one you meet. You'll see their heart's truth and you'll see the poisons they carry within. You have claimed the memory and power of the Goddess you truly are. Use it wisely, be kind and compassionate to your fellow human brothers and sisters. You can now really help them heal."

"I know Dad; I have an inner peace within me that I find strange. My body has no memory of such peace. I need to confront him and terminate the charade he has been playing for centuries. Once that is done I shall return to healing through food and herbs. I shall write the most captivating stories anyone has ever written; for now I have access to the history of humanity and that beyond the realm of the earth." Saraphina sounded strong, sure of herself. She was a new woman, and had found the power she had lost in the sacrifice for the belief in pure love. Now she had claimed it back and could continue with what had been interrupted centuries before. 'To lead the younger brother of mankind to a new future. To live productively and consciously about their immediate environment as they did successfully in ancient times.'

"Ramon!!! We are back; we are back where we left once before. Our life in ancient Peru, before the European invaded our land!" she spoke with excitement.

Ramon laughed and hugged her. "I'm happy that you are back. Welcome Saraphina, as you can see we were brought to our starting point. Brava, you and me; working together once again to lead the world in a new direction. Just timely don't you think?" Ramon laughed and so did she.

Saraphina had a new clarity, a new purpose and clear direction. Now she understood that no matter where her family was, together or apart, they were close, they could communicate instantly through the power of the ancients, their God selves.

Brava was finishing up the induction presentation with some of the new volunteers that had arrived the night before. As she turned to put away her presentation materials her jaguar tooth necklace lit up and she heard the now familiar sound. She turned and saw Putuma, Saraphina and Ramon walking along the river bank. Brava saw that Saraphina and Ramon's necklace also was alight. Brava ran to greet them; Saraphina hugged her little sister and said, "I'm back sister. I'm back with great strength."

Brava smiled and told her. "I'm glad the jungle has brought healing to you. We have so much to do in this world. Now we can do it consciously once again."

Saraphina walked straight, strong and sure footed. It was obvious she had undergone a transformation. The children ran to greet her and noticed she was calm, unafraid and not bothered by the mosquitos or bugs of the jungle. Atticus said, "You look different, but nice different." Saraphina laughed and whispered, "I'm feeling very strong Atticus and I like it."

The camp was alight with celebration that night; everybody including thirty volunteers partook of supper. Marita and Jabaro had made an enormous array of foods that looked delicious, the aroma in the air was mouth-watering. Cooper and Brava made a welcoming speech to the new arrivals and expressed their happiness about the transformation and growth of La Cintura. The future looked promising and life in the jungle was good once again. Cooper asked Saraphina for her permission to keep Atticus for the rest of the year. He could learn many great things in the jungle and perhaps grow to be a great conservationist. Saraphina promised to think about it, she needed to discuss it further with Atticus and make sure that was what he wanted. Brava added "You know we would take good care of him, right?"

Part Three

Step gently but surely,
Walk ahead step by step.
As the journey is never
What you find at the end.

Brava had said good bye with tears in her eyes. She had been so happy to have the family all together at her wedding and the weeks after had been a great way to really get to know each other. Atticus was staying, he was happy to miss out on the boring school days and learn practical skills for a few months. Violet was going to miss him however she was happy to have Saraphina to herself for a while. Saraphina herself was renewed; she was unafraid and strong, and ready to return to the world she had left behind and pick it up with new energy. There were things to be done, books to be written and awareness to be shared. Her work was taking a new direction; her stories had always been about the constant battle between the ego and the soul. Now she had material that would reach deep into the hearts of readers and would fuel them with a passionate motive.

Putuma and Ramon had spent some time talking, making sure they would remain in touch through meditation and telepathic communication. Ramon asked Putuma to be his sounding board when things got complicated. The shaman hugged Ramon with great affection and assured him he would be waiting on his call. Atticus hugged Ramon and cried. He was going to miss him greatly. Ramon asked him to practice his singing by imitating the sounds of the jungle. He had said that he would be expecting a concert of all he learned on his return.

Jabaro had packed his shoulder bag. Marita was hugging him. She was going to miss both the men, she had fallen in love with Jabaro and adored Ramon as the person he was. It was a sad moment of departures, people going in all directions back to where the world needed them to be and some remained where they had been from the beginning. However the Great Spirit has a way to make things happen and maybe from the goodness of its heart would bring them all together once again.

Jabaro and Ramon arrived at the Lima airport with one hour to spare before their connecting flight to Buenos Aires, they sat at the café talking about Jabaro's land. Ramon, even though born in Argentina, had been living outside the country for decades. He knew of the region the Mapuche occupied however he had never visited.

He asked Jabaro about his people and their history, and wanted a little background on them to be prepared for the meeting with their chief. Jabaro gave Ramon a rundown of their history from the time before colonisation.

"The Mapuche are a people that lived in the South of Argentina and Chile for thousands of years. Long before the Spanish colonised our land. Since colonisation we have fought to retain our lands and have dispersed through the provinces of Neuquén, Rio Negro, La Pampa and all the land along Patagonia. We have been persecuted and pushed from our land century after century by the governments of both Argentina and Chile. Our people are on both sides of the Andean mountains. We are the first people; we have stories that go beyond Spanish times. We know we have existed for thousands of years; our legends go back to the time of the great Tsunami. We are as ancient as the Aymara, or the first people of the jungle. Listening to Putuma's stories made me realise how alike we all are, how our brothers have struggled with the same thing ever since the Europeans arrived at our shores. We have been pushed in every direction, always taking from us what they wanted, making promises of letting us have our lands until they decide it has mining potential then they attack us again and kill many of our people till they find a new site for their exploitation. We have stood against the powers that be, over the last four centuries. Our brothers on the Chilean side of the Andes have fought and suffered greatly. In Chile, the Mapuche, which means "people of the land," are Chile's largest indigenous group. They make up 1 million of Chile's 16 million populations. Our brothers have been struggling to reclaim their land in southern Chile for years.

Since 1974, the Chilean government allowed the logging industry to exploit Mapuche land. Today, the majority of the Mapuche's land has been seized and given to multinational corporations. The struggle to regain their land has led to clashes with the police and logging companies. The Chilean government has been using an anti-terrorism law, put in place by dictator Pinochet in order to detain the Mapuche; this is how they classify us, "Terrorist".

There have been many conflicts over time, one of them was in 2002, when police raided a Mapuche village detaining many and injuring others. Young children were killed in the process. The reported tragedy started a new era in the conflict which continues today; where police raid Mapuche villages and detain those with political views under the anti-terrorism law. The police say the raids are part of "preventative warfare."

The results of these raids are brutal for the Mapuche; often beaten or shot with rubber bullets. Several injuries have been reported on both sides of the border, including injuries to children and elderly people. The younger Mapuche have only known racism and oppression from the state. However our sons, the young Mapuche are now the ones mobilizing in an effort to get back their ancestor's land.

Many of the Mapuche that are imprisoned have gone on hunger strikes for long periods of time these have helped draw attention to the struggle. At a recent meeting of the Chilean President with the European Union he was questioned over his commitment to the Mapuche struggle and to human rights. He responded with some garble that had no meaning.

In the coming months, the Chilean government will be prosecuted in the Inter-American Human Rights Court for violations to the Mapuche community rights under the anti-terrorism law. Slowly the Mapuche's struggle is gaining more attention and gaining more support, we shall claim our land and identity back.

The Chilean government has signed several international treaties, including ILO 169, which protects indigenous rights. We need to keep an eye on them and push for the treaties to be implemented and if these treaties are implemented the government will have to give back the Mapuche land and respect our rights.

The Argentinian and Chilean governments need to provide solutions to the conflict and protect the rights of the Mapuche. We are re writing our history and we are demanding that we be respected as the ancient people that we are and not as natives without any rights or understanding of political issues. We have cultural values and ideals. We have our own religion and we had it long before Christianity invaded our shores with the promise of salvation. Our God is the God of the people, we've been saved by him before and his promise to us is that he'll return to save us again."

An announcement over the PA stopped the conversation; however Ramon felt he got the gist of the problem. It was all over again, the same issue he had encountered with the Mamo in Colombia and the governments, the native people had been pillaged and robbed, murdered and raped by the colonists just like animals with no rights, no souls and no value. Ramon felt the sadness of the people in his heart. He felt that it was far too old a problem to be current in today's world. Colonisation had happen five hundred years ago, and people and their societies had grown to be racial bullies and thieves. Ramon thought it would be interesting to see what the Great Spirit had in store for him, as from his vantage point of view he couldn't see too far ahead.

The plane landed at the Aero Puerto Ezeisa in Buenos Aires at 8:30 pm. There were people waiting for Jabaro and Ramon at the airport. A car drove them to the city of Buenos Aires for the night. Ramon thought of Celeste as they drove past places he knew well, places he had spent times with friends on Sunday afternoons and at music festivals and picnics. Celeste was his sweetheart girlfriend at the age of sixteen, he had never made love to her; they were too young and inexperienced to face the decision even though Ramon had tried. Celeste wanted to marry as a virgin, her religious upbringing demanded it. He had seen her years later by accident in a chance meeting while he was in Buenos Aires for business. She was married at the time with two young children. Twenty five years later he was back, they had been chatting on Facebook for a few years. They had reconnected after a very long time. She was divorced now and had grandchildren, so did he. Their relationship online became an inspirational one. There was no talk of anything else but how to go through the next day, or the next issue at hand. They spoke about many things, trivial or important. Ramon had sent her a love letter every Tuesday as his words for the week. It had gone on for five years and today he was so close to her. He was wondering if he should make contact before travelling south.

"Jabaro!" said Ramon. "Do you mind getting the driver to do a special stop for me? It's on the way and wouldn't take long."

Jabaro told him to tell the driver where he wanted to stop. Ramon instructed him on a series of turns and asked them to stop by a little shop, the sign read, 'Modas Mar'

It stood for Mary's fashion, playing on the word Mar for Mary which meant ocean or sea, what she loved most.

Ramon stepped out of the car and stood in front of the shopwindow, inside there was no one, he felt his heart sink hoping to surprise her with a phantom vision, something she would not believe her eyes were seeing. As the thought crossed his mind the door behind the counter opened and Celeste stepped through it into the shop. She looked up and froze. Ramon's eyes met hers and he smiled at her. She ran to the door unlocked it and ran to his arms unable to believe it was true. She hugged him, kissed him, and hugged him again, asking time and again if it was true or had she gone crazy and was imagining it. Ramon laughed and assured her it was true.

They kissed in the middle of the footpath uninterested in who was looking. Ramon told her he had no time to stop now but wanted to let her know he would be in the country for a few weeks and he would be in touch about spending time together.

"I may need your help again" he said with a smile that meant an opportunity to spend time alone.

He took her number and promised he would ring later, once he was settled in. She looked over his shoulder and saw the Mapuche natives in the car.

"Are you here to help them?" she whispered as she hugged him good bye.

"Yes, there is work for me to do with them in my birth place, the Great Spirit has brought me here and I'm excited at the opportunity to help my native brothers with their issues, just like we did with the Mamo, remember?"

"Yes I do, the best time of my life and it's still going strong. Let me know what you need from me. I'm so glad you are here, I thank the Gods for bringing you back to me and those you are about to help."

Ramon kissed her and got back in the car, they drove off to continue their way. Jabaro asked in a humorous voice.

"Who is the Babe?"

Ramon laughed and told him how she came to be in his life. "Her name is Celeste, she was my childhood sweetheart, we haven't seen each other for twenty five years, but have been in contact through social media. She has been very instrumental in helping out with the Mamo and their issues. She manages a website with updates on the progress of the recognition of their indigenous rights and the watch over the Colombian government sticking to their promise. I'm sure she will be a great contact to have when the time comes for us to raise awareness of what's happening here with the Mapuche and their human rights. I would like to spend some time with her if there is time before we travel down south." Ramon looked at Jabaro waiting for his reply.

"We leave the day after tomorrow, early in the morning. We have a few hours' drive to our land and perhaps you can organise to meet tomorrow, she seems to like you a lot!"

Ramon smiled, "There is a fondness we have maintained for a long time, and thirty eight years is a long test for anyone. A moment alone together could bring happiness to both our hearts. Thank you, I shall call her later and organise a meeting place." Ramon went into his thoughts for a while. As the images of the city passed by the window his mind travelled back in time to their youth. To the first time they kissed, her shaking nerves and all the expectations they had of themselves at the age of sixteen. It had been a long journey for both of them; the thought of being able to spend time together in a hotel room was tempting; he so wanted to consummate the love that had been waiting for them to have a chance. Now older, less inhibited and experienced he was sure they would not waste a moment. Celeste was intelligent, and had been involved in the matters of the world of the Mamo from afar. She was persistent, had an eye for detail and encouraged him to go further. Ramon was feeling that he would have a moment to be a man, just a man with the company of a woman, not a world saviour, or a hero. He needed to be humble, small and vulnerable in the privacy of their meeting.

Later that night, when everyone had settled down and had discussed the details of the trip down south to Patagonia he found the opportunity to ring her.

"Hello Celeste, me again."

"Hi my love, how are you! I'm shaking still; I can't believe you are here in Buenos Aires. So close and yet I'm not able to be with you." She said with a shaky voice.

"That's why I'm calling; we won't leave until the day after tomorrow, can we meet? I have a large room in the hotel Hermoso in the city, would you be able to come and meet me?" Ramon was hopeful he was not intruding in her life, she like him was a busy woman, and he had turned up unannounced.

"Yes, I can come now if you want, I don't think I'm going to be able to sleep tonight knowing I could be with you, even if we just talk all night." Celeste was eager to be with him.

"Will you be alright to drive into the city? There is parking and we are off the Avenida Colon, it should be easy to get here from your place," he said.

"Si, si. Yes ,Yes I can come now, I don't want to miss out on a minute if possible. I'll gather a few things and will leave right away, txt me the exact address please," she said as she began to collect personal items and stuff them in the bag.

"Yes, I'll do it straight away, so I guess I'll see you in an hour or so!" he said excitedly.

"Yes an hour, lookout for me. See you soon", she said and hung up the phone.

Ramon felt nervous and excited at the same time. He knew he would not sleep; they had so much to talk about and catch up on. He decided to go and tell Jabaro that he may not be up in the morning and that if there was anything important to do he would be in touch after lunch. Jabaro smiled and said for him not to worry, everything was taken care of and that he hoped enjoyed himself in the reunion with Celeste.

The traffic was calm, as the peak hour traffic had died down and the roads were clear. Celeste drove thinking of the time when they saw each other last. She was so young, married and loyal to a husband that had not been much of a man to her or the children. However she was loyal, she didn't want to mix things up and Ramon had understood and respected that. Today she was a different woman, she had been independent for years now and there was nobody that demanded accountability from her, she was free to come and go as she pleased. She laughed at the thought of the orange; the first time they kissed and he put his tongue in her mouth she almost vomited. She thought it was gross and disgusting. Ramon had looked at her and asked how did she learn to kiss? She smiled and responded that she had practiced with an orange. An orange!!! laughed Ramon at her. She responded innocently that she had seen it done on the TV soap-opera's and practiced it with an orange, "why?" She defended herself. Never mind he had said, I'll teach you. Just relax your lips and let me kiss you gently, everything will happen naturally; you'll see. She laughed as she drove on, thinking of how innocent they both were, and how he would respond to her tonight. Would he be critical of her kisses? Would he find her fat, or old? Years had gone by and she had no idea if he had been with anyone lately. She tried to shake her negative thoughts from her mind and instead think of how wonderful it was that they were meeting again.

Ramon had been looking out the window, keeping an eye out for her. He saw her car pull up at the curve of the road and ran down to meet her. She was locking the car when he got down stairs; she smiled and dropped her bag on the floor to embrace him. They kissed for a moment and he spun her around like a child once or twice and picking up her bag led her to the lift. Once in the room they sat to admire each other. They talked about the Mamo, what was happening in that front and how people were still joining their cause. Celeste asked about the Mapuche and what were they going to do? Ramon responded that he had no clear instruction on the issues at hand but soon he would have a better idea. He would let her know if there was any help he would need from her. After a while of conversation the stars in their eyes burned brighter and their hands and bodies got closer. They kissed and enjoyed their time alone. Ramon took her to the bed and laid her down; with gentle kisses and exploring hands he discovered her sensitive places. Her breathing got deeper and faster with every caress, clothes came off her body piece by piece landing on the floor. Soon their bodies were skin to skin, naturally naked touching one another, feeding off each other's warmth. Celeste wanted all of Ramon, she had waited a long time for him to come back and now that they were together she wanted him deep inside; feeling his pulse, his blood rushing, his breath on her neck and his kisses. Ramon equally eager mounted her, entwining his arms below her back to take a stronger grip and entered deeper still. The warmth of her inner thighs and the wet penetration into her depths was almost an instant ejaculation. He kept still waiting for the sensation to subside, he wanted to last for ever, he wanted to take her to the doors of heaven and show her the light. She kissed him, biting at his lips, looking into his face taking in the vision, the weight, the moment of action. Something she had imagined many times before but had never done in the flesh. His eyes puffed up with the heat of love and his lips fat with the bruising of her bites made him more irresistible, she wanted to eat him; to keep him and never let him go again.

Ramon began to push again, slowly moving back and forwards, reaching deep into her womb and holding back his orgasm. He spoke words of love, he told her how beautiful she was, how beautiful she had been and how much they had missed out on. In the next breath he said that it was better now than when they were young, now they knew how to find pleasure without assumption or expectation. Now was a time when one surrenders to the pleasures of what each other wants; serving oneself of that pleasure, seeking it and helping oneself to achieve the highest climax unafraid of ego or selfishness. Ramon reached his climax as Celeste bit his shoulder and scratched his back with sharp finger nails. He closed his eyes and saw in his mind's eye the light, white light of heaven, ecstasy and pleasure they speak about in the Kamasutra. Celeste watched his face as he ejaculated and that brought her to orgasm also making her cry with ecstasy and pleasure of finally consummating their love.

They lay next to each other laughing uncontrollably like teens; they remembered the orange kiss, and made fun of their innocence. They looked into each other's eyes and said more than words could ever say. They made love again and again that night, each time getting higher into the realms of ecstasy.

Ramon lay watching her breathing, the rise and fall of her belly, the mountains of her breast and her golden hair cascading down her shoulders. He thought of how life seems to keep gifts for some time later. Moments that appear when one believes that all opportunity has been exhausted.

At six am Celeste got in the shower, packed her belongings and kissed him good bye. She had to open her clothing shop and was hoping to have dinner that night with him. Ramon kissed her intimately and promised to organise for her to meet Jabaro so they could know each other and have a connection for when it was necessary. She was happy with that.

Midmorning Ramon met with Jabaro, they had breakfast together and Jabaro told him about their meeting with the chief of the Mapuche the next day, "It will be a long drive to the south and we'll be arriving late in the evening, but they are eager to meet you Ramon. Our chief is the head of our society and we have other people of high rank that will speak with you. I will be proud of the moment when we arrive and that I have delivered you to my people completing the task assigned to me by the elders."

Ramon smiled, "I'll be happy to meet them too. Is it OK to invite Celeste to our dinner tonight, I would like you to meet her so that we can have a contact in Buenos Aires, someone that knows the kind of things I need. She has done plenty for me before in similar situations and we already have an established platform."

"Yes by all means, bring her to dinner, it will be nice to meet her and see who is the owner of such a man's heart," laughed Jabaro.

"Great," said Ramon. "I think you should understand that the only one that owns my heart is the Great Spirit. Everybody else just gets a chance to share it for a little time."

That evening they dined in the usual Argentinian style, late dinner at eleven pm, customary to the people of the big city. They sat to an array of barbequed meats salads, bread and wine. The people at the table conversed at length with Celeste, about her interaction with the world through the internet platforms raising awareness of the Mamo and their human rights conditions in Colombia. Celeste impressed them with her knowledge of the current situation the Mapuche were experiencing in Argentina and the outcry of their brothers in Chile. Celeste also mentioned how she had heard that most Mapuche Indians in Chile were treated as if they were invisible, having no rights to apply for jobs or career paths in many professions. Jabaro spoke about how in Argentina the situation was very similar and that most indigenous people were only able to get domestic work for the females or farm hand work for the men.

Jabaro looked at Ramon and said, "I can see why you like her, she is a woman informed about the worlds issues" and embarrassing Celeste said "Great to know you Celeste".

Celeste felt accepted and she could feel the beginning of a new chapter unfolding in her life, this time closer to Ramon and his work.

That night Ramon and Celeste made love once again and talked until the small hours of the morning and promising to keep in touch about anything he needed from her. In the morning she left early again, this time with a passionate kiss that showed her happiness to be with him once again. Ramon watched her go down the stairs; she blew him a kiss and disappeared through the car park door.

Part four

When road is long
And your destination unknown.
Keep your ears open,
For in the wind you'll hear the way.

Ramon packed his bag and made his way down to the breakfast area, where he waited for Jabaro and the driver to come down. He was ready to learn more about the Mapuche and be among them. Before he met with the men he logged in to his email account to see if he had news from Brava in Peru or Saraphina back in Australia. There were many emails from friends and other people interested in Ramon's healing workshops and others asking of ways to be part of La Cintura. Ramon forwarded those to Brava to take care of the reply and recruit new volunteers to her vision. Brava had sent an email that touched Ramon's heart, in it, she stated how much she had learnt to love him and how she was missing him already. She felt abandoned, but she was being selfish, for she loved him dearly. She understood that he had to help others, especially the Mapuche brothers. She had seen firsthand what he achieved with the Mamo and what he helped her achieve in Peru with the neighbouring tribes. She apologised for making him feel guilty for going to Argentina and just wanting him with her. I have become accustomed to having you around Dad, Atticus misses you greatly even though he is having a lot of fun and learning great skills. He has found a baby sloth and made him his pet. Gato misses you also; he looks for you every day and spends time smelling the air to see if you are coming back. I hug him for you and he understands, maybe you could come visit him through the power of the medallion. Cooper and I are doing really well, we work together and feel closer than before we married. The number of volunteers has tripled and we are finding ourselves booked out for the rest of the year. We are planning to buy more land and build more huts and a larger kitchen for Marita. By the way she sends her love and asked to pass her regards to Jabaro.

I shall write to you every time we are in Puerto. Hope you have access to a computer where you are. Love you Dad, stay safe and return to us soon. Blessings. Brava. Xoxox

Before he could open the email from Saraphina; Jabaro and the driver turned up and asked Ramon if he was ready. Ramon logged off and followed them. The drive from Buenos Aires to La Pampa was long; they started off at six am and drove through many remote parts of the province of Buenos Aires, farms of wheat and other grains and cattle Tambo's all along the way to La Pampa. The terrain was a flat green valley, the humidity of the central part of Argentina was heavy and the water-filled lakes plentiful. As they drove along the road that led them to La Pampa, Ramon spotted a turn off sign that said Bolivar and he was sent into a memory flashback of his days in the Navy. Once a month he would travel with Lucho to Bolivar to see his parents. Lucho was his friend and comrade in all sorts of escapades. The life of the Navy had given them discipline and safety amongst a government that was dangerous at the time. The military coup of the seventies had killed many people, anyone with political ideals was in danger and the 'report a neighbour' policy introduced by the new government had worked amongst the citizens of Argentina. The campaign was about reporting any activity that may be suspicious and if one happened to have enemies one was in danger for the Dob in campaign was anonymous. The Military killed over twenty five thousand people; their only crime was having a political view. Entire families disappeared and today the effect of that disappearance is still a scar in the hearts of the people of Argentina. Ramon remembered hearing about what went on in the Navy School he was in. The dungeons of the school were torture chambers where many were raped and killed after a parade of military personnel had their way with them. Bodies had been washed up along the coast of Rio de la Plata. Bodies still alive in groups of ten or twelve tied together and dropped into the deep river to drown. Body parts dismembered washed up all along the coast line. Toddlers and infants were taken from their families and sold to overseas buyers. The fate of these children was never known. Ramon felt his stomach tighten, the thought of being there again brought memories he thought had gone for ever. However the past always comes to haunt the mind of those that suffered, no matter how deep one buries the memory. He remembered the fear his family went through whilst the military coup was in force and he never wanted to experience that again.

They stopped not far from the border of the province of Neuquén, where most of the Mapuche people had settled after they had been pushed around by the Spanish. The town was a gathering of small houses in an isolated part of the country. The terrain had changed dramatically and the green watery valleys had become arid deserts. Ramon wondered why they had settled there as not far from their land there were much better pastures and water access. According to Jabaro the reason for it was because the government was not interested in deserts so the Mapuche were left alone in these parts of the country. The people came out to greet the travellers. The Chief, a medium height man with strong bone definition came out of one of the houses, he wore a skin over his shoulders that showed patterns painted and stitched on it. Ramon took a good look at the figures that adorned the inverted animal skin that seemed to keep the Chief warm. Small geometrical shapes of diamonds and square crosses equal in length, and others that resembled waves in a continuous pattern. The Chief came to greet Ramon with open arms; his eyes looking deep into Ramon's. Who bowed gently thanking him for his invitation.

Jabaro spoke in native tongue with the elders and the Chief while Ramon listened and found the sounds made by the Mapuche interesting. So much so that he could not think of any similarity with any other language he had ever heard. The Chief took Ramon by the arm and led him to the house; there they offered him refreshment and a light lunch. Ramon and Jabaro sat to eat, the others looked at them; Ramon felt uncomfortable eating under the pressure of such an audience but soon they moved to the outer part of the house and sat to talk when the Chief asked the others to leave them alone as he wanted to talk to Ramon about business. Ramon looked out across what seemed to be an endless horizon of red dirt flat land and a blue sky that had no mercy on the shadowless earth. The Chief asked Ramon how things had turned out in Peru and Ramon gave him a run down on the issues they faced there. How his daughter Brava had successfully gained help from the local tribes to protect the forest and animals she so much cared about. She had made La Cintura Research Station a strong presence on the border of three countries and the immediate communities there. He spoke with much affection about his daughter and how she had started, how she worked alone for three years and built a camp to house volunteers with interest in her vision. Today La Cintura is known all over the world and she deserves all the credit for such achievement.

The Chief listened attentively; he was taking in every word Ramon spoke. The Chief asked Ramon about his understanding of the Great Spirit and how he worked with such energy. Ramon explained that he had had a series of events through his life that seemed to be related to everything that had happened in his life over the last few years. He spoke about receiving the invitation letter to go to Colombia, how he had met Don Ignacio and Don Yuco and things had developed from there. Ramon told the Chief about the black line, the walk for one hundred and eighty days of offerings along the black line, about the keepers of the earth and the things he learned from the Mamo. How they had initiated him over a series of arduous tests and rituals and how the medallion he wore was an amulet to open his mind's eye and communicate with spirit. Ramon spoke about how Don Ignacio had found his daughter and brought her to Colombia so both could meet for the first time and how he had been following their lifelong journey and knew everything about them.

"I miss and love Don Ignacio very much, he has passed to the world of spirit and now when I need him, he comes in spirit to help me understand what to do when I can't figure it out alone." Ramon spoke with emotion in his voice.

The Chief then spoke with equal calmness. "We heard through our neighbours that there was a man in the north of the continent helping native people gain their human rights, access to culture and their existence. We've seen things through the internet, films about the talk in London and the thousands that came to witness the speech of the Mamo, we saw you standing next to the Mamo and decided then that you were the man we needed to help us. Jabaro told me that you were born in Argentina, so you are a brother of ours. You would know about the political situation of the country and its history, would you not? He asked Ramon and waited for an answer.

"I have lived outside Argentina for decades now; I have learned more about my birth country from outside its borders and was able to be more instrumental because I understand how the world responds to causes like the Mamo or the Amazon Rain Forest. People who have access to the technological commodities can speak the language of the developed countries. People in the developed countries have a need to embrace the remote, the rare, and the less fortunate. These people are great donators to causes that assist the less fortunate or the oppressed to attain what they need. That is the tool I understand, being outside Argentina made me an instrument to our South American brothers. Knowing how to appeal to the masses and reach out to them is what I discovered I can do well and coupled with a handful of friends that are devoted to my work, make it successful." Ramon stopped talking and turning to the Chief asked.

"Chief Anibal, what do you want from me?"

The Chief looked at Ramon and lowering his gaze thought for a moment, then he looked into the distance of the horizon and continued.

"I was named Anibal by my parents, "Anibal" do you know what that means or its origins?" he asked Ramon.

Ramon answered with a brief "No"

The Chief continued, "It comes from Hannibal, a great warrior that threatened the Roman Empire and made them shake with fear every time they heard his name.

It means Grace of Ba'al (God) in the ancient language of the Phoenicians.

I don't know how or why my parents chose that name for me, but it is for sure that I have not been able to make any body shake with fear when they hear my name. So you see, I need to make a difference to our people. They haven't had a Chief for many years that has stood and claimed the culture of the Mapuche, someone who stood strong for the rights of his people and demanded that the world respect their ways, culture, language and arts. I think about it day in day out. I carry in my heart a sadness that weighs me down. I see how our beliefs have been torn apart by the writings of men that spoke about us as mere natives with very little knowledge and nomadic existence. I want to bring back the respect, the pride of being a Mapuche. We were forced out from our lands over the mountains to this part of the earth, we intermarried with the Puelches and adopted some of their customs as they absorbed some of ours, then as we spread and moved along Patagonia mixed and married the Pehuenches and the Araucano blood took other strands of lineage making us the Argentinian Araucano Mapuche. The Mapuche from the other side of the Andes

Mountains are of a different strand, they have Aymara lineage and have spread through all the south of Chile. Our ancestors came over the mountains long ago as the Spanish pushed them off their land and they had to move away trying to escape the constant harassment. So what I want you to help us with Ramon, is to make the world notice us, help us let the world know of our identity. Who we are and how long we have been standing the terrible push and shove that we suffered from the moment the Spanish landed on our shores. I want my people to be proud of their blood lines, culture and beliefs."

Ramon had listened carefully to what Chief Anibal had said; he picked the words that were poignant and meaningful. 'Culture, art, language and traditions' and thought the similarities experienced by the cultures of native people all over South America were the same. Governments had failed to take care of the first people, the original people of the land and foster their culture but instead they had been proactive in weeding them out, eradicating the native blood without a second thought. Ramon felt a sort of rage welling inside his stomach. He could not comprehend how five hundred years of colonisation had not changed a thing for these people; they hadn't been able to integrate even though they had tried. The Mapuche had sent their children to be educated in schools for a better future, not only to make things easier for many of the younger generation but also to be represented with informed well-spoken Mapuche that understood law and human rights. All this had failed somehow. Ramon needed to think about things, he needed to have some time alone, space to think to listen to the Great Spirit that had brought him here. How to go about it, what to do?

Ramon found an opportunity to walk alone along the dusty road that seemed to go on into infinity. Nothing around it could be seen for miles. It seemed that after spending so many months in the Rain Forest here he was sent to hell, where nothing grew, not a tree could be seen. The sunset was a blaze of orange in the sky. He could distinguish a greenish glow on the horizon line, he wondered if that glow was caused by the shadow of the Andean Mountains. He held his medallion as he thought of Don Ignacio, asking in his mind for enlightenment about the situation at hand. He felt the medallion glow, he heard the sound that came with it and soon he could hear Don Ignacio's voice in his mind.

"What seems to be the matter Ramon" asked the voice of Don Ignacio.

"Don Ignacio, thank you for responding so promptly. I have spoken to Chief Anibal and have heard what he wishes to achieve with my presence here. However I'm having trouble understanding what to do about it. I wish I could come up with an idea to assist them. It is obvious that they have endured much segregation and its time they are accepted and respected as the original people of the land, but I don't yet know how to go about it. Maybe it's the isolation I can feel here that stops me from thinking better, or more creatively. I pray you will be able to enlighten me on what to do." Humbly asked Ramon.

"Remember how it took you many weeks of walking the black line with us, making offerings and seeing how we endured the hardships we had in our way? Well here perhaps it's the same. You may first see what these people experience, understand who they are and I guarantee you that the answer will come to you like a fresh rosebud that awakes in the morning dew. Trust that you are here because you have what they need. The Great Spirit never puts us anywhere without reason. Trust Ramon, Trust." The voice faded away and Ramon felt alone again.

The sun was touching the edge of the horizon and the light was fading gently, as he turned and walked back to the town, thinking that perhaps it was better to give it sometime before coming up with suggestions. That night he sat around the table listening to people talking. They were telling stories about their Gods and Ramon felt absorbed by the story, as he had never heard it before. One of the older ladies was telling it to the children who sat by her.

"Long time ago, there was a battle between the two greatest creatures in the world! The God of the sea Kay-kay, a half serpent half fish monster that was making war on Xeg-Xeg God of the mountains and controller of volcanos and domain of the earth. Kay-kay yelled out kaikai!!! And as he uttered those words a great tsunami wave rose in the sea taking all humans and living things in its path, turning them into sea creatures and keeping them there for eternity.

Xeg-Xeg seeing what Kay-Kay was doing raised the land into the shape of great high mountains to protect the humans and give them shelter high above the ocean waters. The humans ran up the mountains but many died unable to escape the force of the tsunami, others survived to tell the story that has been passed on from generation to generation for centuries. All the people that survived gathered on top of the mountains to thank and pay respect to Xeg-Xeg. They sang and danced so much that their footsteps flattened the mountain peaks and today those flat tops are sacred places of ritual and offering. Xeg-Xeg told our people that he would return to help us when the time comes and that we should run up to the flat tops of the mountains where we will be safe when Kay-Kay returns. The ancient people of our tribe say that all those of us with a marine second name are direct descendants of those that died drowned by the tsunami". The old lady pointed at some of the children and said, "So you Marino, Concha and Delfin are descendants of the people that became creatures of the sea."

The children were speechless, their eyes wide with the effects of the story, their imagination still active with the images the elder portrayed in their minds. Ramon was equally struck. He had never heard that story and it seemed to be so familiar, so similar to many he had heard before, about the way countries started in many places and continents. He thought for a long time about the story, he wanted to make sense of how creatures that looked like snakes were responsible for creating such effects on earth and its people. The Aztecs had feathered serpents in their mythology. The Mayan also had serpents of colours and feathers. The Aymara believed that a feathered serpent came from the sky and they were direct descendants of such creature and even across the world in an isolated land mass the size of a continent the Australian Aborigines' spoke of a rainbow serpent the creator of the world. The people of India and Sri Lanka have stories of two great serpents dividing the land in a fight for a Princess. Where did all these stories come from? He wondered. There is such close proximity in belief systems from people who had never heard of each other or even seen other lands, somehow it's all so alike, the same roots. Maybe that is a good point of approach, how similar people are in their respect for roots and identity and the supreme.

That night Ramon rested comfortably in a small room on a comfortable bed. His body tired, from the long drive, a long day and many hours of conversation. His mind was exhausted and he was happy to surrender to the God of Sleep Morpheus. He wished in silence that Morpheus took him in his arms and rocked him like a babe, so that he could rest deeply and safely. The night seemed to be still, and Ramon was soon asleep however dreams had been waiting for him to be available so they could enter his mind. In the dream Ramon saw a road up ahead, red dirt, dusty and isolated. He was dressed in white, odd he thought for such a place. As he noticed the cross roads up ahead he looked at the enormous horizon line that extended for ever with nothing to be distinguished upon it. As he approached the cross roads and turned right, a few steps later he sees a woman riding a bicycle without the use of her hands. He noticed that the shape of the woman was grotesque, shapeless a tall mass of black material that seemed to entwine itself around the figure, only allowing her eyes to be visible. As she rode past him she looked with piercing eyes at him, a strange sense ran all over his skin. When he looked back to follow her direction she had disappeared. As he walked on, he distinguished a rock protruding out of the ground, the shape of a fang tooth about a metre tall, on its side near the top a small opening like a cave. He looked inside and saw that there was an eco-culture living there, muscles of large size stuck to the wall of the small cave, water and algae that looked healthy and happy in such secluded environment. Ramon looked at his surroundings again and retuned his gaze to the small cave; not believing what he was seeing as he was standing in the middle of a desert. Next as he walked on, out of nowhere a young man, native in appearance walked past him wearing a black suit, looking impeccable in such dusty terrain. He was baffled with such occurrences. Ramon awoke in the dark room; his dreams showed him a collection of strange images that made no sense, at least no sense at that moment. He wondered what messages it would convey eventually.

The next day he rose early, he was sitting outside on the veranda by the time the Chief joined him. They drank Mate, a traditional Argentinian drink made of green tea leaf, ground and served in a small gourd, drunk through a metal straw until the sound of the empty vessel lets the drinker know he or she has finished the drink, then returned to the server for refill and passed on to the next person. Mate is a very social drink; it brings people together and creates reunion and conversation. Ramon had been thinking about the dream, his eyes fixed on the dusty road ahead. He went over and over the images, and as he thought, he realised that it had to be related to the people of the area. He noticed that the road he saw in the dream was very similar to the one he was looking at. He asked the Chief about a crossing of roads nearby. He offered more detail saying, "A place with pointy standing stones"

The Chief thought for a moment and then added that there was a road a few miles down that was strewn with rocks of a very sharp and elongated nature. The crossing of the two roads took one to the west or the south. "Why do you ask" said the Chief.

Ramon dismissed the question with a comment, "Just wanting to know, I had a dream last night and there were the crossing of two roads. That's all"

The Chief announced that the Machi, the medicine woman of the tribe was coming to see him. She had heard that Ramon had arrived and wanted to meet him. "She is a very powerful woman" said the Chief. "She has great ability to see spiritual matters, I believe she reads the thoughts of people"

Ramon took note, he was cautious about people reading his mind, he had experienced it before and it wasn't a comfortable feeling. Don Ignacio passed no judgment about Ramon's thoughts but the Machi could be different. After all they had called Ramon to help them out, disregarding her power.

A group of Mapuche youngsters walked past with a herd of cattle, behind them a monk walked talking with another young Mapuche. Ramon looked at them and asked the Chief, "Who are they?"

The Chief responded saying, "They are the Salesian monks, they have been here for over a century and have taught the Mapuche how to better their crops and breed better cattle. They have taught us how to read and write for decades and are great musicians. Do you know Ceferino Namuncura? The chief asked suddenly. Ceferino was trained and educated with the Salesian monks; he was a great singer and student. He was our eyes and ears; able to interpret what the Spanish men said to us."

"Come look at his picture" the Chief got up and walked into the house leading Ramon to his room. Above the bed there he was, the picture of the young man he saw in his dream, wearing a black suit, combed hair, young and immaculate. Ramon felt his skin crawl, he suddenly remembered his childhood. He knew Ceferino, they had met before and there had been three occasions he could recall. Ramon was beginning to understand the dream, pieces were coming together fast and of their own accord. Ramon stood in silent thought, the Chief prayed whilst Ramon stood gazing at the picture, then he walked out of the room inviting Ramon to follow.

Outside they could hear greetings going on, the women in the house were chatting and the Chief turned to say to Ramon, "The Machi is here" and winked an eye at him.

Ramon collected his thoughts and prepared his mind for the introduction to the Machi.

Buenos Dias Machi! Good day Machi!

Buenos Días Jefe Aníbal, como está usted? Good day Chief Anibal how are you today?

Mira quiero que conozcas a Ramon Rochette, el Chaman que ha venido a ayudarnos.

Look here, I would like you to meet Ramon Rochette, the Shaman that has come to help us.

The Machi looked into Ramon's eyes intently and intensely. She looked deep into his soul and when Ramon felt she was about to read his thoughts, he thought of a wall of lead, a gigantic wall of lead that stopped her mind penetrating his. Ramon did not know where the image came from but it seemed to work. He saw in her eyes a strange expression as if she had been stopped from entering a temple. Something she had never experienced before. She greeted Ramon and told him she was happy to have him help the Mapuche people and would work beside him in anything he needed. Ramon nodded and thanked her for her warm welcome.

The Machi's name was Nora, the Chief left them to talk alone. Before he walked away he suggested to Ramon that he spoke to Nora about the dream he had had. The Machi and Ramon chose to sit outside on the veranda, where the air was fresher. A young native girl brought them mate, she would come and go every few minutes to refill it with hot water and bring it to the next person. Ramon told Nora that he had a collection of images shown to him the night before through dreams. "The one I want to understand the most is an image of a woman riding a bicycle along the road. The image was not right, it was a mass of black material wrapped around what should have been the body of the person riding the bicycle; however there were no arms or legs protruding from beneath the material and the only thing visible were her eyes. She looked at me intensely and I felt an icy look from the creature as she rode by. When I looked back to see where she was going she had disappeared."

The Machi listened attentively; she smiled and made a grunting noise, just like she knew what it was instantly then she asked Ramon.

"Did she say anything to you?"

"No! She rode by and looked into my eyes with a hard cold look in hers" said Ramon.

"Do you know much about our legends? Our mythology let's say" asked Nora.

"No, not really, I learnt something about the creation story, or the Kay-Kay and Xeg- Xeg legend, but that's about it so far" responded Ramon to her question.

"Well we have many legends in our mythology, we are an ancient people and we go back a long time. There is one that is the most fearsome of all, the story of Peuchen. Peuchen is a demon if you like a creature capable of shapeshifting into anything it likes. It can use the shape of any animal to attract its victims into a trap, and then converting itself into something horrific turns into the beast that it is and consumes the victim's blood. Other times it has been known to turn its victims into stone. If one looks into its eyes, one can be petrified on the spot.

I think that the woman you think you saw in your dreams is Peuchen checking in on you! I'm sure the demon already knows you are here and has come to see what powers you possess. I must advise you to be careful as it will try to lure you away into an isolated place and take you or kill you" said Nora with urgency in her voice.

Ramon listened with interest, he wasn't afraid of an armless bicycle riding woman wrapped in a large quantity of material. He smiled and responded that he would give Peuchen a run for its money if it came to it. "So is it a he or a she, male or female?" he asked.

The Machi, responded that it was what it wanted to be at any time. "We just call it Peuchen, which embodies everything it signifies."

Ramon thought for a moment about the image in the dream, her eyes. They were certainly female, encased in an outlined set of eyelids almond in shape. The colour was a mix of grey blue and green, glassy and cold. If the Peuchen was already thinking of keeping an eye on Ramon, he questioned its motives; he was there to help the people that believed in it. So why would the Peuchen be feeling threatened by him being there?.

Nora continued speaking about other things amongst which she brought up the inability to read his mind or thoughts and said that it was the first time she came across someone like that. She could always look into a person's head and see what they were all about. "What intentions they had arrived with"

Ramon smiled and felt comfortable about her comment, he preferred that. He said that he could not explain why she couldn't read his thoughts; perhaps it was that his teacher Don Ignacio had taught him how to protect his mind from the powers of others. Or perhaps it was something necessary to be safe around places with Peuchen's running lose! he smiled at the Machi.

The Machi smirked but not with pleasure, she smirked with the disregard she felt coming from Ramon about her warning. "I shall tell you one more time. Be careful of the Peuchen's tricks. If you go looking for it and you disappear don't expect me to waste my time looking for your carcass."

Ramon reached over and held her hand; he smiled and told her he was joking. It was interesting that he had come across many spirits, but never had he been told about anything like the Peuchen. He would like to hear from Don Ignacio about it, and maybe he could go for a walk sometime and commune with the spirits of the desert. He was sure to get some advice from them.

The Machi finished her serve of mate and stood up. She asked Ramon to come by her house in the next day or two and she would continue discussions with him and perhaps tell him more legends about the Mapuche beliefs. Ramon agreed to pay a visit and continue the conversation at another time. The Machi left and Ramon returned to talk to Chief Anibal.

"Chief Anibal, what do people do with the priests from the Salesian order? Do they learn things; do they run a business, what kind of activities go on there?" Asked Ramon trying to gather understanding of why would they have settled in such a remote place.

"The monks teach our children to read and write, they are the school of the Mapuche, and they also learn to sing. The Salesian monks have a great choir and our children sing like angels. Also they teach us to improve our stock by mixing the genetic pool with other breeds, resulting in better quality meat and milk. They have been kind to us and have protected us. Some of our people learn how to use computers and other equipment so they can be more competitive in the workforce" responded the Chief.

"Do you think that the monks are keeping the Mapuche traditions alive, things like legends, history, language and customs? Or that they are absorbing the Mapuche at a young age and making them believe in a God other than the one the Mapuche believes in." Asked Ramon once again.

Anibal, the Chief thought for a moment. "We speak about our legends to our children; you were witness to that the other night at my house. We speak our language at home so that our children grow knowing their native tongue. We have many festivals that celebrate our culture and legends, our God's and our ways. The monks take part in it and enjoy our activities and we don't think they are trying to change us in any way. I believe they are trying to give us tools to survive as a tribe and a nation of people. Our young are able to represent our people in political situations and rallies and they even know how to write to the government about our situation, addressing our concerns and any political promises that have not been maintained or kept."

"I just wondered if the Mapuche were losing their natural instincts because of the education they are acquiring from the monks. It's all well and good to have great intentions, however the danger is thinking that "Our way is better" educating the native people found in remote lands simply because they don't have your cultural understanding; therefore education of an European nature is introduced and not the other way around. Learn the culture of the original people of the land and try to communicate with them in their way, understanding what is important to them. They were there first, and they had ways much older than the ones introduced by colonisers. Don't you think?" asked Ramon to the Chief.

The chief thought about what Ramon had said for a moment and then spoke again.

"I see what you mean. Yes I believe there is danger in the introduction of an education system foreign to ours, however we have fought against the Coloniser for centuries and have not achieved much and they impose laws upon us and make regulations and land divisions that impede our freedom. We managed to keep our culture going for all this time, we have our ways still being exercised today and keep passing on our stories to the younger generations. There comes a time when one must decide to learn enough of the foreign ways so one can fight them with their own law. That is what we are trying to achieve now Ramon; we want to find a way that makes the people of this country wake up to our rights and not dismiss us as natives that aren't important in today's socioeconomic world. We are the ones that will survive when Xeg-Xeg comes to help us; not the colonisers."

"Ok", said Ramon. "I shall think of a way to make the people of this land be respected, there has to be a way of making them important, a national pride. The Mapuche pride. It's time we let them know that enough is enough and the Mapuche shall not be pushed out of their lands anymore."

That afternoon Ramon walked along the dusty road alone, he wanted to think, to get a feeling for what could be done to bring awareness to the people of Argentina about the Mapuche situation. As he walked he thought to himself about how he had raised awareness about the predicament the Mamo in Colombia were experiencing. The world had responded with kind support in so many ways; todays humanity know that unless the people take action and stand for what its right, governments only partner with big companies for profits. Native titles, and native rights have suffered much over the centuries and it was time they got what was theirs in the first place.

His thought about the Mamo in Colombia took him straight to Brava, his beloved daughter. He felt so far away from her, he had enjoyed being there fighting and working with her to build a strong border resistance against poachers and deforestation. The arid ground around him only reminded him how far away they were from each other. His mind missed them all, his heart softened with the memories of seeing them together at Brava's wedding; he laughed at the memory of Sarapina's first impression on Marita, covered in a black mosquito net from head to toe, making such an effort to walk that she face planted on the river bank. They were all doing alright he told himself. Perhaps it would be good to see Brava through the mind and pay a visit now to surprise her. Ramon sat on the sand; he adjusted his hat so the sun glare wouldn't be too bright. Holding his medallion he thought of Brava, the camp and Atticus. In seconds the medallion glowed and his mind's eye came into focus, he was back at the thick Amazon Forest, he saw Gato walking toward the tree where he liked to rest. Gato smelled the air and stopped, looked around and growled as if calling him. Ramon walked up to the cat and patted him on the head, around his ears and spoke to the big feline.

"Gato!!! I miss you so much! I loved being with you in the forest and talking about things. How are you?" asked Ramon. The cat who could see him in spiritual form spoke back.

"Ramon! How long are you going to be away for? I, we miss you too, and Atticus is driving me crazy, that kid never stops. Gato come here, Gato do that, Gato, Gato Gato!!! Take him with you. I'm getting too old for so much running around!" Gato was pretending he didn't like Atticus, when in truth he was missing Ramon.

"Are you sure you are annoyed by Atticus, or is it something else?" asked Ramon now rubbing Gato's chin.

Gato rubbed his face on Ramon's chest and walked away. "You better be back soon!" he said seeing that Brava had spotted the behaviour he was displaying from her hut. She ran to the spot where Gato had been talking to Ramon, not seeing him but sensing that Gato had seeing something there. Ramon touched her arm and spoke in her ear. "Hold your necklace and come to the river bed." Brava felt the words in her mind and did as she was asked. As soon as she held the necklace she began to see fragments of Ramon coming together, until his image was fully visible.

"Dada!!! How are you? Oh how I miss you!" she said with tears visibly showing.

"I miss you too!!! Look where I am now!" he moved his hand and as if opening a window she was able to look at the open desert that spread for miles.

"Wow a bit of a contrast isn't it?" She said. "How is everything going there?"

"Good, the Mapuche are a very interesting, a well suffered nation of people. I have to come up with something to help them and perhaps bring awareness to the world about them, for now I'm only listening and working out what we can do to change things." Ramon looked at her and smiled, he then asked "How is married life?"

"Great! We are doing so much, please when you finish with the Mapuche please come back to help us out, we are working hard and there is so much interest in everything we do. I had three reporters come from magazines, one of them from Melbourne; to do an article on me. Tara has been amazing and it is because of her interview and article that all this has followed." She was happy and she looked strong.

"Great, that it's what you wanted darling, this will keep on growing and La Cintura will be a model example for future conservation movements. I'm so proud of you. How is Atticus doing in the jungle?" asked Ramon missing him also.

"He has taken to Cooper; they spend lots of time together. Cooper sees him as his little brother; perhaps this is good practice for when he becomes a father!" Brava smiled and Ramon asked.

"Are you planning to start a family?"

"One day" replied Brava.

"Ok, don't do that to me, you know I'll know when there is a life engaging with the earthly body of my daughter, right?" Ramon smiled at her, thinking that she was so young and so beautiful.

"Stop it Papa', you will make me cry, hate to tell you but I can hear what you think. I'll be alright but don't leave me too long, at least when you have time come visit me just like today. I see you and Gato have reacquainted!" she finished.

"Yes, I miss him so much; here there is not much else other than birds and spirits that do funny things to people. It's interesting but if I had Gato with me things would be more fun. My darling I have to go, I cannot leave my body unattended for too long there is a spirit here that likes to play tricks on people and I must be careful for now. I love you, be strong and know that I'm with you every day." Ramon caressed her face and began to fade.

"Thanks Dad, I love you too! See you soon!!!"

Ramon opened his eyes to a bright sun above him, the dust blowing across the road had settled on his lap. He stood up and walked back to the house thinking of Brava.

Part Five

Still, strong and steady,
See what's in front of your eyes.
For illusions are mare tricks
Played by your mind.

As Ramon continued without thinking about how far he had walked, he heard the cry of a baby. He looked around and there was nothing to be seen, no housing, no people just a few low shrubs that grew out of the dusty terrain. The cry was persistent; he walked around following the sound until he came close to a crevice about two meters deep, the sound got louder and he scurried down the side of the crevice to the bottom of it believing the child was there. As he looked around for it a loud voice spoke in his ear.

"Wanting to do good are we?"

He looked around to see who had spoken but there was no one to be seen.

"Finding yourself a little confused Shaman, are you?"

Ramon knew instantly that it was not a human voice; he knew he was in a predicament and perhaps it would be a dangerous one. Ramon held the medallion and thought of all the nature spirits; with it came a blue light that engulfed him, like an aura, a glow that kept everything outside its space and magnified what was lurking nearby. The voice spoke again.

"I see you've got friends in high places! Are they strong enough to help you right here and now?"

Ramon asked in a calm voice. "Who are you and what do you want?"

The voice responded with laughter, sometimes like the laughter of a witch and sometimes like the most childish laughter one could ever wish to hear.

"What do I want? Who am I?" and the laughter followed.

"I am the legend in person, they call me Peuchen. You have heard about me have you not? And what I want is to know what are you doing here so tar trom what you know?" asked the voice still without a physical appearance.

"I was invited here by the people of this land, what is your business with me?" asked Ramon.

"I want to know what your interest in saving the Mapuche nation is, there have been many that came with promises of help and have left with their broken promise and a worse situation than they found in the first place." said Peuchen with a patronising tone.

"I was invited to come here by the people of this land. I've heard what they would like from me, what they face; and I've come with no promises. However I shall try to do something about it. Is that a problem for you?" asked Ramon.

"I have a problem with little shamans who think they know much about nothing. I want to see how you deal with some little experiences I have prepared for you."

As the voice of Peuchen said those words the light turned to darkness and a spinning sound filled Ramon's head. Clouds of colour and lightening spun around him and he didn't know if he was spinning around or if the cosmos spun around him. The voice was now just laughter in the air. Ramon held his medallion tight; he could see the glowing aura around him still with brilliant blue light. Moments later or what it seemed like a length of time hard to measure the spinning stopped and a forest of light appeared. Enormous trees rising into the sky rose from the ground, light of different hues made the trunks of these trees. The foliage was feathery tear drops of light that shimmered and glowed as they fell to the ground making a carpet of colour that moved as the breeze blew them away. Ramon felt he was alone but being watched, the voice was silent and there were things that lurked behind the beautiful trees. He knew this was a test and any enchantment would be broken as soon as he was enamoured with it. As he thought so it happened, there were figures that ran and hid behind the trees, there were sounds of voices and whispers around him. Ramon stayed still just watching what happened around him. The voice spoke again and this time was calm and of a liquid texture.

"This is the Petrified Forest Shaman; we have been here for this long! We are ancient people; legends speak about us, about the creatures of the Forest, Duendes!!! And other beings that kidnaps and steals children and lonely passers-by never to be found again. Look at them! Can you see them Shaman?" asked the voice of Peuchen.

Ramon was watching a group of children running around playing what it seemed tiggy. They laughed and chased each other.

"The people of your world know nothing about the Mapuche people. They speak about the Mapuche as mere natives with limited understanding. They fear us Shaman, they disregard the people but fear us! You see how can that be possible if you turn a blind eye to one thing but not to others? They segregate the Mapuche but keep their legends, give life to a world of underworld creatures that will come to steal their children and enchant the adults. They run away from the Petrified Forest because staying here at night would be just crazy. The Duendes or Leprechauns as they call them will take them and rape them. Hahahhahhhahahahhaa" the laughter of Peuchen resonated through the magnificent light forest. Ramon was calm and observant.

"I've got something to show you Shaman" said Peuchen.

The forest made of light disappeared and the arid desolate place it had become over centuries returned. Ramon was standing next to a forty foot long petrified trunk of a tree that lay on the sandy ground. He could distinguish tracks made by visitors to the park that day. The forest he had seen in etheric form was not there to the tourist that would visit, however as Don Ignacio had told him many times, all that it was exists as a blue print of everything on another level that never leaves or disintegrates. Ramon watched what had become of such a stately forest, ancient vegetation that stood once thousands of years ago. The people of the land had seen it, lived in it and sheltered under its canopies. Today only a few petrified, crystallised logs remained, however the power and myths survived amongst its people.

The Chief had looked for Ramon everywhere, he had sent men to comb the open grounds for him, night had fallen and Ramon hadn't returned from his walk. The full moon was in the sky making the open country easy to scour however there was no sign of Ramon anywhere. The Machi heard of Ramon's disappearance and she sat to look for him with her mind's eye. As she dropped oil droplets into a bowl to assist with her vision she felt her skin crawl. She had a strange sensation and she knew instantly that the visiting Shaman had encountered the Peuchen out there alone.

"I told him to be careful! I told him that it was keeping an eye on him. He didn't listen." She spoke out aloud to herself as she shook her head.

She sent word to the Chief of it, telling him that it was only a matter of time until they found him again or came across his bloodless body. The Chief was worried, he thought of the danger of the Peuchen and its ways. He knew that no one came back if the Peuchen came across their path.

Ramon not thinking that his host would be worried about him missing from the house continued watching what the Peuchen showed him.

The vision of the light forest came back and he was standing once again looking at the children play. The Peuchen stood next to him; it had the body of a goat and the face of a turtle with human eyes and mouth. As it spoke, it changed form constantly from one combination of grotesque and unimaginable animal to another. Ramon had trouble keeping his head straight as the constant shapeshift was too much for his mind to accept.

"Are you having trouble Shaman? Is my nature and power giving you a head ache?" The voice with patronising tones had return.

"I wish you would choose one shape and stay with it, it would make things less distracting" responded Ramon.

"You don't seem to be too afraid of me are you Shaman?" asked the Peuchen in a whisper.

"I would pose a question to you" said Ramon. "You claim your power from people's fear of the legends and that gives you the energy to exist; is that correct?"

"Yes, you are correct, human fear is what makes us real, their energy feeds us and we come alive with it to satiate their need to be afraid" said Peuchen.

"I know that the Mapuche have no written language, they have borrowed the Spanish alphabet to interpret their sounds, so there are no books that speak of you or any of the other forest creatures I can see and hear. So if this is true and you only have life because you are spoken about by people who fear you. Wouldn't you think that you should fear the disappearance of all legends? The Mapuche younger generations are leaving these lands and integrating into the westernised societies? Aren't you afraid of being forgotten? If you are forgotten you will not exist anywhere isn't that a concern for you Peuchen?" said Ramon now patronising the myth.

Peuchen was obviously angered by his comment, and a strike of lightning broke through the sky above the forest. "I shall suck your blood and leave you for the vultures to feed on your carcase" screamed Peuchen.

"You will do nothing of the sort", said Ramon. "If you think for a moment and consider what I'm telling you, you would make sure you return me safe to the road where you found me. You would help me with the cause of the Mapuche and would make sure you tell me great stories so that I can use them to instigate curiosity among the people of Argentina and perhaps the world. That will give you and your friends here no matter how ugly or scary, life to go on and exist for centuries to come. Isn't that a better idea Peuchen?" said Ramon calmly.

Peuchen smiled and came close to Ramon's face. "You speak wisely Shaman, I'm not certain that I like you or your lack of fear, but your words have great meaning." Peuchen shapeshifted again and with a call that sounded like a bird call gathered all the creatures of the light forest around them.

"You've heard what the Shaman has said; do you think there is wisdom in his words? Or should we feast on his blood and teach him and others a lesson?" said Peuchen watching Ramon's face to see if it could find fear in his eyes.

The creatures murmured in a muddle of sound and then went silent, no one spoke a word. Peuchen turned to look at them and said, "I see you find wisdom in his words and it is obvious you want to survive, erasing memory of that which we are is a way of killing us all. Very well I shall return him to the road. Shaman we shall meet again."

With that came a swirling of colours and a sensation that made Ramon's stomach turn as if he was spinning fast and was about to be sick, suddenly his eyes were looking out into the distance at a moon that was about to set on the horizon. Dawn was coming and a new day beginning. Ramon walked into the kitchen and the cook almost dropped the pan she was holding, she gasped and spoke words of surprise at seeing him walk in.

"Dios mio! Don Ramon!!! My God! Ramon!!!

She ran to call Chief Anibal leaving Ramon in the kitchen. He looked at her reaction and wondered what had happened to the woman. Chief Anibal ran into the room and hugged Ramon. "Thank God you are alright", he said and hugged Ramon again.

Ramon apologised for being out all night without telling anyone. He said he had a very interesting night and that he had learned a lot about some of the legends of the Mapuche culture.

The Chief asked, "Were you taken by the Peuchen?"

Ramon smiled and nodded; the cook made the sign of the cross and prayed. Ramon felt odd; it seemed that people were worried more than he anticipated. Chief Anibal took him by the arm and walked him to the veranda, asking the cook to serve mate.

"Tell me what happened? Are you alright? Did you see it? asked the Chief in low voice.

Ramon told him no detail, he said that he had met with the Peuchen and that she had used a spell that removed all notion of time and he didn't know for how long he had been gone. Ramon didn't want to talk about detail, he needed to process what had occurred and understand it, and then he would talk.

"Chief, I met with the Peuchen, she, for it's a female most of the time. She tricked me and confronted me. We spoke about a few things, she showed me things that I need to assimilate and process before I tell you much more. There is some understanding of what it means. I promise that I shall tell you soon. Everything is alright we came to an understanding in the end." said Ramon, buying time.

"Ok, Ok. You tell me when you are ready, I just wanted to make sure you are Ok, no one had ever returned and we are amazed that you have. The Machi saw you in her vision with the Peuchen, sent a message to us and we looked for you till late at night. We came back after we heard from her", explained the Chief.

The Machi came running and as she approached the veranda from the road she started talking. "You escaped! You escaped the Peuchen!!! She laughed out aloud; she ran up the step and checked Ramon over.

"I saw you, I saw you with the bad energy of Peuchen. She tricked you; didn't she? I warned you!!!" she said as if scowling him.

Ramon laughed and hugged her. "I'm glad to see you as well!!!" He laughed again and told her that he wanted to talk to her about serious matters. She went to lead him to her house as the cook brought him a serve of mate.

"Not right now, let's have mate with Chief Anibal and we can have a little discussion between the three of us." Ramon smiled at them.

The Machi sat next to Ramon waiting for him to talk, to tell her everything he knew. "So are you going to tell us something about what happened?"

"Well it was the Peuchen as you said that appeared in my dream, she was keeping an eye on me. It's a she, even though she changes shape she is always the voice and mouth of a woman, her eyes are also female. She came to my path and spoke about fear and tried to terrify me with things she would do to me. She used magic to transport me to places and see creatures that were horrific in shape, and at the same time she showed me the tenderers images of children at play, laughing. She was erratic and her continual shapeshifting made it difficult to concentrate on what she was saying. A lot more happened but my head is full right now and I need to rest a while and think before I can go on telling you what happened." He said sounding tired now.

The Machi spoke next with interpretation. "We were afraid of it, a she you say?" Interesting she murmured. "We never knew it had a gender, all we knew is that she is powerful and feeds on the lives of those that fall prey to her ambush tricks. There had been many that disappeared and children too!!!" she said with a glazed look as if recalling a memory.

Ramon said as if following her vision. "I saw them there"

The Machi looked at him with questioning eyes then continued. "I've heard of many more creatures that come from the underworld to fetch a victim." As she was about to take a breath to continue, Ramon interrupted and asked if the Petrified Forest was nearby? Chief Anibal and the Machi both looked at him with questioning eyes and asked at the same time, "Very far!!! Why?"

Ramon snapped out of his mind's eye and saw them look at him strangely. Oh!!! I asked just because of the Duendes! the leprechauns, the ones that are known for the rape of humans and the kidnappings in the legends. They say they are found in the Petrified Forest. So how far would you say it is from here?"

At least three hours by car! and that is driving very fast!!! replied the Machi. "Did she take you there?" she asked strongly.

Ramon laughed, "Be patient, I shall tell you everything when I have rested, let me process it. I'm going to lie down for a while and sleep. I shall seek your company later in the evening." Ramon got up and left for his room.

The Machi and the Chief stayed talking for a while longer. Ramon could hear them from the veranda, debating about possible things he had seen. He laughed at some of them. As he listened exhaustion and a tired body took the better of him into a deep sleep. Dreams and visions came and went through his mind and absorbed by a tunnel of light that sucked him through a rainbow wormhole, he arrived at the peak of a mountain. As his eyes focused into the vision in front of him, and adjusted into perfect definition, his awareness was heightened and as his new reality settled, he saw himself from a birds eye view and from his own eyes, as if he could see in every angle at once. Realising where he found himself, all focus was brought to an enormous snake, larger than he had ever seen. The serpent slid down the side of the great rock and came to coil itself around Ramon in a circle with the head as a hood above Ramon's head; as if protecting him from all harm. As the serpent finished entwining itself a great energy rushed through his spine and kundalini was set free. Ramon saw then not with the eyes, or the mind. He saw for the first time with the eyes of awareness; consciousness of a depth not understood by the brain. He met Kay-Kay the protector of the Mapuche people; the God that had saved them once before from the tsunami of Xeg-Xeg and promised to return to save them once again if necessary. Kay-Kay had given Ramon its blessing, its protection and acceptance. With it, Ramon was assigned the responsibility to be its intermediary and do Kay-Kay's work in the world of man. Kay-Kay and Ramon communed for a time of no importance, as time is irrelevant in the world of energy. They understood each other and Ramon was shown visions of what to do, the end result, and each step to take. Kay-Kay touched his medallion and the blue stones shone white, then pink and eventually blue fading in a pulse rhythm till it glowed gently on his chest. Ramon at that moment saw the world from outer space, then from close proximity and in an instant he heard every mind and every thought of every human on earth. He listened until he felt the white noise fade away and only the heartbeat of humanity remained. His eyes filled with compassion for the little blue rock and its people. Ramon's eyes opened, he focused on the ceiling of the room where he had laid down to rest. He felt the glow in his chest and the energy of immeasurable proportions in his mind, his awareness. He sat up in the bed and tried to breathe deeply two or three times, then stood and walked a few paces, straightened himself and walked out of the room to the veranda. No one was there, the sun was almost setting and there were voices in the distance. Ramon walked to the kitchen and helped himself to a glass of water. He saw a note pad near the fridge and a pen. He took the pen and drew a serpent, noting the patterns and the colour he thought it was. He put the piece of paper in his pocket and walked to Nora's house a few hundred meters away. Nora the Machi, was sitting in the kitchen drinking mate and reading her own cards. She heard him come through the gate and got up walking to the door. Ramon smiled and she greeted him with contentment, he was back to tell her everything.

"Como has dormido?" "How did you sleep?" she said.

"Bien, bien gracias." "Good, good thank you".

"Actually" said Ramon following with intention to go straight into the dream.

"Can we have some mate please, my throat is dry and I wouldn't mind some."

The Machi served him mate and encouraged him to go on.

"Machi!, sorry Nora! I just had a visit from one of the most highly regarded Gods of the Mapuche people!!! I've been blessed by the God of the land Kay-Kay!!!

Nora looked at him with an expression of surprise and ignorance at the same time, not following his thread of conversation.

"When I left you and Chief Anibal, I lay down and heard you talking for a moment then suddenly I was gone into a dream world. I remember feeling as if I was falling, but also being pulled through a tunnel of rainbow colours, so many colours!

until I arrived at the top of a mountain. The top was like a flat surface, as if someone had cut the top off or stomped it down. Then my vision was from everywhere at once. I could see me from far away, from above, below and sideways. I could look inwards or outwards. Suddenly an enormous serpent came down from the side of a huge rock and slid past me just so I could see how large and gigantic it was. It turned to look at me came back and coiled itself around me, making a shelter around my body with its body and with its head, provided me with a roof. Then there was light a light, of brilliance that took all form and made it disappear. Only the awareness of being was there and knowledge of everything we have to know manifested itself in my understanding. I saw Kay-Kay and it spoke to me about saving the Mapuche people, his people once more as he promised long ago." Ramon was crying, not knowing that he was as he spoke.

The Machi, cried louder and going on her knees took Ramon's hands and blessed her head with his hands. She sobbed asked for forgiveness and she repeated the words a few times. Ramon taking note of her apology, held her face and asked why was she asking for forgiveness from him? The Machi responded that she had been suspicious of him from the moment he arrived at the town. But she had been wrong and she had committed a sin as a medicine woman. She was blinded by her jealousy and envy of him being asked to find a way to help the Mapuche people and not her.

"She was a Mapuche and the Machi of the Mapuche, she should be the one to find a way." she said to him. "Now Kay-Kay gave you its blessing and I know that it's you that came to helps us, selected by Kay-Kay itself. Forgive me Ramon" she cried at his feet.

"Nora! Nora no! no, no!!! There is nothing to forgive. You were cautious and that is a good thing. I'm here because I was told to come. But I'm here to work with all of you, and you will be the most instrumental one for the work Kay-Kay wants to achieve. You are part of the solution. I need you to be my right arm and trust me with what we will have to do in the next few months. Will you Machi?" Ramon asked with a smile.

Nora got up and sat on the chair; she wiped her face and controlled her tears.

"I'm so blessed to work with you!!! she cried again unable to hold back her tears.

"Good", said Ramon. "Now I'll tell you about Peuchen!!! You are going to love it. This is getting really good, you guys are amazing. Your culture is so alive and so everywhere that it's becoming fascinating. I must say you are very passionate, you all are. You move fast and waste no time. Sorry I got a bit excited, I think its Kay-Kay's energy going through me that makes me this way. Well! I was walking along the road and I heard the cry of a baby..." Ramon told her the whole experience, he left no detail out and at the end he told her he had a plan and that the Peuchen was agreeable to it.

"We are going to hold a celebration, 'A Festival to Peuchen' and all the legends of the Mapuche people. I want to do it out in the fields, open space lots of space and bon fires and I want every Mapuche to be present. We will wear traditional clothing and everybody is going to be proud of being a Mapuche Araucano!!! That is the spirit of it. Can we organise it for a fortnight's time?" Ramon asked the Machi.

"A festival to Peuchen?" said Nora in surprise. "People are terrified of it, especially now that she took you!!!"

"I understand, remember its Kay–Kay's plan. People will have to come; we'll talk to the town", said Ramon.

Chief Anibal was consulted and he made decisions that a meeting of the people was to be held that week. During the following days Ramon prepared the Chief and the Machi for what was going to happen. He explained that the people would be fearful of the legends and that there should be dances and music that expressed these legends as a sort of invitation for Peuchen to be present.

"Fear gives the legends life. And we need the fear of the people to give them life however they must remain in the field and not run away. It's a confrontation they must endure and be strong to stand. I shall do things that will show them magic and spiritual work first hand," said Ramon to the Chief.

"I shall make sure I explain it to them at the meeting and give them detail of the way they should perform on the night," responded the Chief.

Ramon looked at Nora, and asked if she could make sure that the dances and music were suitable for the occasion also that she prepared some ritual to bring the consciousness of the Mapuche to a heightened awareness. She responded positively.

Ramon took every chance to walk alone on the road, revising his plans for the festival. He held his medallion and called on Don Ignacio, Don Yuco and Putuma the Shaman from the Amazon. They made themselves present, whether through telepathy or vison. Ramon told them to look into his mind and be updated on what was to occur on festival day.

"I know it's a big task to perform, the Peuchen and the Duendes are to show themselves that night. It's a risk we are taking and hope that Peuchen stands by her word. Could I ask you to be available on that night and make yourself visible to all people present including the Legends? I'm going to need all the help I can get" said Ramon to the Shamans.

Putuma was the first one to respond. "I shall be in trance state so I can be present, I shall manifest beside you Ramon, that shouldn't be a problem."

Don Yuco, who had not spoken to Ramon for months, was happy to hear from him. "Ramon, so glad you are working hard to help our brothers from down south. I shall make sure I'm present and shall stand beside you at the ceremony. Looking forward to sharing the experience of the Legends of the south, with you."

Don Ignacio appeared beside Ramon, walking along the road, step by step in time with Ramon's pace. Ramon walked and looking at Don Ignacio's feet, noticed the Old man didn't leave foot prints on the dusty road.

"I believe you have found a way to assist the Mapuche Ramon" said Don Ignacio.

"Yes, I was blessed with the vision of Kay-Kay an ancient God, the keeper of the people and the land. It gave me instruction on what to do, and it will work through me for the benefit of the Mapuche. I have confronted the Peuchen face to face and we have an agreement that encourages joint forces about preserving the history and legends of these people." Ramon spoke with renewed confidence.

"I told you things present themselves when we are ready; see how you have arrived at a plan of action! The Great Spirit never leaves us in a difficult place without a plan of his own to rescue his instrument. I shall be beside you standing tall, as a spiritual brother and assist when necessary Ramon, you have my word." Don Ignacio disappeared as the echo of his voice remained in the air.

A few minutes later Ramon noticed a large bird flying toward him, as it came closer it changed from a Condor to an eagle and then a pigeon. Landing in front of him it shapeshifted once more into the shape of a dog with camel legs and the neck and head of a llama. Ramon laughed and said, "You really have fun doing that, don't you?" he asked still laughing.

Peuchen rolled her eyes and responded, "No matter what I do you don't seem to fear me. It takes all my energy reserves to make myself visible to you! I wish you feared me a little bit so I could stay longer." She made a sad face as if following his jolly nature.

"I have news for you! We are celebrating the legends of the Mapuche culture and we are creating a festival called 'The festival to Peuchen' in your honour!" Ramon looked at Peuchen with a broader smile.

Peuchen had no expression, she didn't know what to think and excitement and happiness was not something she practiced in her nature.

"A festival in my honour?" she repeated in a surprised voice.

"Yes, in your honour" responded Ramon.

"How interesting, I may not be able to contain the desire to steal some of the Mapuche people or children, you do trust me too much Shaman!" said Peuchen looking at him with blue eyes almost softened by his action.

"Peuchen, its important you don't do anything of the sort. The people will be afraid, very afraid. It is a celebration of the Mapuche legends so that you and your world have plenty of energy infused to keep on existing. This fear shall empower you for a time and will refuel the stories that the people of this land shall speak of for a long time. You must appear to them and speak to the Chief, make a pact to protect the Mapuche culture and its history; then you shall be celebrated every year, bringing renewed energy to your world with the stories being passed from generation to generation for decades to come," said Ramon to Peuchen.

Peuchen sort of smiled a shy smile. She didn't want to be too nice to the little Shaman, however she was happy with his plans of a celebration of the Peuchen and its creatures.

"Fine Shaman, I shall control my desire to eat some of the people, and I shall give instruction to all the creatures of the underworld about respecting the celebration and not kidnap any children or maidens. Be sure to make it big, we are fearsome and would not be happy with a little celebration lacking in effort or energy." With it she vanished.

"I shall call on you again soon" yelled Ramon into the air. Ramon returned to the house. He saw the monks walk past with the children and the cows and thought of the work they did and how dedicated they seemed to be to the Mapuche. He walked into his room to add some notes to his notebook and as he looked up trying to go over the things to remember he saw at the end of his bed kneeling on the floor with hands raised to the sky Ceferino Namuncura. Ramon gasped in surprise. He looked at the door and then back to the image, however Ceferino had vanished. Ramon thought hard about what it could have meant. He knew that the Chief was a devotee of Ceferino and the Mapuche loved him, but why was he appearing to Ramon? He tried to write some notes, but his mind kept on flashing images of Ceferino kneeling at the end of his bed. He then remembered when he was a child about nine years of age the same image had appeared in his room beside his bed. At the time he got scared, as children do with anything extraordinary. As he thought about it, he remembered two different occasions where Ceferino appeared again. Only on one occasion he wore something different, other than the black suit he was always portrayed in the images of the church. On that occasion he wore a Poncho, a Mapuche poncho, now that he had seen them up close. Ramon realised that so many years ago Ceferino had shown him something in the future. Ramon laughed in surprise and spoke, "I'll be amazed if this doesn't work" everything was coming together as a plan that had been made long ago and Ramon was just a pawn in the game, an instrument that brought things together in the material world. That night as he slept he dreamt of Ceferino, again he was wearing his black suit but this time Ceferino spoke to Ramon for the first time.

Part six

Remember your dreams
Listen to what comes to mind.
For all things occur
At the same time.

"I'm a Mapuche that followed the ecclesiastical education of the Salesian monks. I started singing at a young age in the choir and fell in love with the notion of God, the Christian God of the church. Not because we had no God of our own, no. We are very devoted to our Gods; I believe that our own faith made it easier to be of better service to the Christian God. My health was weak from a young age and my people had great expectations of me, especially my father. He was the Chief then and I his son, who was to be educated to be the interpreter for our people. As time went by I became more and more absorbed in the Christian faith and as my health deteriorated the Salesian Monks took me to Italy to recover. There God called my name and I left the body and this world," said the Saint.

I believe you were canonised in the last few years and now you are Saint Ceferino Namuncura, the people of the Catholic Church worship your name and ask for favours in exchange for prayer is that correct? asked Ramon.

"Yes Shaman, that is correct. I was always devoted to helping the people of the land, and anyone that called upon my grace. I have blessed the fervent faith of those that pray with pure hearts and bestow miraculous healing on them. Because of these claims to my grace I was proclaimed a Saint and today Christians from all over the world know me and San Ceferino Namuncura. My people claimed my remains so they could bury me in our land. I guess it's a way of identifying themselves with me or through me that gives them a sense of belonging in the new world." said Ceferino.

"So you are the first Saint of Argentina, and perhaps South America! I see how this fits. Have you come to enlighten me in this knowledge so I can proclaim the Mapuche pride on the tenth anniversary of your beatification?" asked Ramon excited with the thought that completed the plan of the Mapuche pride.

"I'm a Mapuche Indian, may I be now a Saint or a Hero as they have proclaimed my virtues. I'm The Lily of Patagonia, the Saint of the humble at heart but most of all Shaman I'm a Mapuche. If you think it would ignite the hearts of my people with pride then go ahead. They need to feel they are worthy people and a culture to be preserved. They have given their own son to faith and through me claimed high rank in the world created by God, Christian or Pagan. Kay-Kay is no lesser a God than the God of the Bible. For in prayer it is the purity of invocation that heightens the seeker of divinity and opens the doors of the heart and the mind to its grace." Ceferino blessed Ramon, and gently dissipated into the ether.

Ramon felt light and happy, Ceferino had spoken to him and explained part of the reason he was to include the Mapuche pride on the anniversary of his beatification celebration. The Mapuche Saint would be the logo that stood for all natives of South America, brothers in faith, sufferers of colonisation and brothers of endurance throughout five hundred years of oppression. Ramon was happy, he smiled at the God's for always having a plan; a plan that once he as an instrument accepted, fell into place all alone. Ramon couldn't wait till morning; he sat up taking notes, writing letters for Celeste in Buenos Aires, with instructions about contact names and numbers. He began writing down the steps to a campaign that would spread like fire through Argentinian soil, lighting up every heart of the South American people.

Early in the morning not long after dawn Ramon sat at the table drinking mate alone, the cook walked in and was startled to see Ramon there. He served her a mate and passed it to her. She smiled and took it from his hand with a shy thank you. He smiled broadly. She looked at him with suspicion as it was too early for anyone to be so happy. Ramon drank a few more serves of the mate and when Chief Anibal walked into the room he was also surprised to see him already there.

"I've got so much to talk to you about Chief Anibal!" said Ramon hardly containing his excitement. The Chief smiled and patted him on the shoulder, "It looks like you've had a good dream" he said sleepily.

"Oh more than a good dream Chief, it was a blessing, my heart is so full. Your culture is so rich in mythology and elevated Saintly beings that my heart has been experiencing a height never before explored by my spirit" said Ramon with a broad smile. The Chief asked for some breakfast to be brought to him outside. He led Ramon out by the arm as he usually did. Seated on the veranda Ramon began telling him what had happened.

"Chief Anibal, last night I had two events happen to me in my room. First I saw a vision of Ceferino kneeling in prayer at the foot of my bed. I looked away and back to it but it had gone, that made me think about what it meant and brought memories of past visons I have had of him. Then in my dreams I saw him again, he spoke to me. A one on one conversation and he told me he is the Mapuche pride, he is a Mapuche first, that happens to be a Saint of the Catholic Church. I asked him for permission to make him the banner of the Mapuche Pride March and he has given us his blessings!!! How good is that?" asked Ramon in an excitement that was hard to contain.

The Chief looked at Ramon with kindness and enjoyment about his passion and happiness; however questioned him about the Mapuche Pride March.

"The Mapuche Pride March? What is that Ramon? asked the Chief.

"Sorry Chief it's something that came to me, I have come to the realization that on the 11 of the 11 of 2017 is the ten year anniversary of his canonisation, his first decade as a declared Saint. We are going to march on Plaza de Mayo on that day and celebrate our National Pride, the only South American indigenous Saint of the Catholic Church. I have been writing to Celeste, my contact in Buenos Aires to organise the march. She will organise for all the churches in Buenos Aires and perhaps the country to celebrate San Ceferino on that day. We will march in our native costumes and carry banners with the image of Saint Ceferino and beneath his portrait the words. 'Mapuche Pride, Mapuche National Pride day.' What do you think?" asked Ramon to the Chief.

The cook who had been listening from the kitchen came onto the veranda with the Chief's breakfast; she made a comment that showed support.

"I think it's a great idea. Our Ceferino is our pride and so it should be that he is Argentina's pride also."

The Chief looked at her then at Ramon. "You are on a winner Ramon, I think that is the best idea I've heard in a long time. We have not celebrated San Ceferino since his canonisation in 2007 when we were present in Chimpay to witness Pope Benedict XVI and Cardinal Bertone performing the beatification. Yes I agree with the march, we are building up on our pride levels and I begin to get excited about being the Chief that led the Mapuche people to be recognised and respected by the whole country." The Chief's eyes welled with tears of emotion.

"Tomorrow night at the peoples meeting can I please ask you to address the people with strong command, show them how proud you are. They will feel it and will be recharged with pride themselves. Tell them about the importance of being there at the festival of Peuchen, about celebrating culture, about looking their best in their traditional costumes and putting on their best performance and dances," asked Ramon of the Chief.

"Yes Ramon, you are inspiring me to write a speech like I have never done before through the years of my leadership. I shall make sure I inspire the people to come alive and be proud, to have a celebration like never before," concluded the Chief with a smile.

Ramon got up and left the Chief to finish his breakfast, he told him that he was going to visit Nora the Machi and talk to her about preparations and a talk from her to the people. The Machi was coming out of her room when he knocked on the door. She opened the door and smiled at Ramon inviting him to come in. She said with surprise in her voice. "I guess you have something important to tell me!"

Ramon smiled and whispered close to her ear, "Always Machi", he sat by the table and watched her get the mate ready. She brought the thermos to the table filled with hot water and began serving the mate. Ramon waited for her to be ready to hear what he had to tell her; the Machi looked at him and nodded giving him a sign that she was ready to pay attention.

"Go on" she said.

"Last night Nora I had a great vison. San Ceferino came to me and spoke for a while about the Mapuche Pride, I have told Chief Anibal the whole story and we have come up with an idea to celebrate our culture nationally..." he went on with all the detail, the plans, the contacts; how they were going to organise it from so far away and how he had contacts in Buenos Aires.

"I need to ask Celeste to come down for a few days; she is my right hand in Buenos Aires and has helped me before in similar matters also she knows what I need from her and she acts promptly. I need a house a small house for her and me whilst she is in town. I need time alone with her and the Chiefs house is too small for us. I would prefer to be somewhere else, more private." he said to Nora.

Nora looked at him with a squint in her eyes. "Be careful Shaman I think I begin to read your thoughts! And you don't want that" she laughed out loud.

"I think I can organise something for you. There is a small place with two rooms by the monks quarters; perhaps you could stay there whilst Celeste visits" smiled the Machi again. "I think that the idea of a National Pride March is a great one and I get to go to Buenos Aires and see the beautiful city that it is. Yes, yes I support the idea. Tomorrow night are we speaking about the march also?" asked Nora to Ramon.

"No, not yet, I want them to focus on the festival of Peuchen, I need their uncertainty, their fear so that Peuchen can have better strength; for now just talk about the festivities at hand," replied Ramon.

Nora was happy, the Shaman had proved to be useful in their campaign and it was proving to be inspirational for all Mapuche. She liked the way he spoke about "US" as if he was a Mapuche himself. He never separated them from him. It was moving for her to see a perfect stranger take so much interest in the issues of her people. He was better than most and she blessed him from the bottom of her heart.

The Chief was writing a speech by the time Ramon got back to the house. He was inspired and wanted to fuel the hearts of his people. Ramon left him to it without interruption. The Machi also felt inspired and made some notes about points to be mentioned at the peoples meeting the next night.

Ramon decide to walk along the road to the church and see if he could speak to the monks about Ceferino and what they could offer as help for the march in the big city. He needed the right contacts, or at least a starting point. Since the Salesian monks where responsible for such honour bestowed on the Saint, they should be interested in participating in the March and celebration. Ramon took the letter he wrote to Celeste with him, he wanted it to be mailed to her immediately, hoping that she would be able to send a message of a possible trip down to him soon. The letter had stated what he planned and what he needed her to organise.

'My Dear Celeste,

It's once more that I ask for your help and assistance. I would like to ask you to take a drive down to La Pampa and spend three days with me. I long to see you and hold you again. There is so much I need to share with you. As usual the Great Spirit has asked of me to do his work and represent the people of the Mapuche Nation in a grand way. I need you to begin working with me immediately and start organising a great event in Buenos Aires. The experiences I have had since arriving here are too many to mention on this humble piece of paper, however there will be hours to talk about it and so much to show you. Hoping you can be with us soon, please send message to tell me of your arrival date.

Love always Ramon.'

The Salesian Monks were welcoming. They had heard he was in town and some had seen him outside Chief Anibal's house. They found Ramon's interest in San Ceferino inviting and were kind in giving him information. They spoke about how the Salesian order of Don Bosco were proud of their Saint and how the moment of canonisation was a highlight for many in their ecclesiastical order. Cardinal Tarcisio Bertone was honoured to conduct the beatification. They suggested he left it to the monks to organise the celebrations of the ten years of the blessed Ceferino. They would contact their dioceses and spread the word so that all churches in the country would celebrate on the same day and perhaps have San Ceferino's banners up for the fortnight before the celebration day as reinforcement to the congregations and the people's faith. Ramon thanked them, his gratitude from the heart. The monks were kind and organised, they were good to the Mapuche and had done a lot to help them and share new skills with them.

The next night the people met, Chief Anibal wore his costume and traditional regalia, the Machi was dressed in full shamanic costume, with head dress, feathers and rattles. She planned to chant and clear the meeting space of evil energies as encouragement to set the mood. Everybody turned up, young and old, there were hundreds and also the Salesian monks were there. The Machi spoke first. She swirled her smoke puffs around her and shook the rattle. She chanted and spoke commanding words to the spirits about protecting the people and creating a sacred space for the meeting. When she was done she yelped a chant and was joined by all present, a call and response method. She moved to the side and Chief Anibal took the stand, he composed himself and with heart felt emotion began to tell a story.

"I remember being very young, a child of about five or six. My Grandmother would tell me stories about our legends, about the Mapuche history like Kay-Kay and Xeg-Xeg, about the Duendes, Leprechauns and Nymphs; about the Petrified Forest and great big animals that roamed the land long ago in our Patagonia. I grew up being afraid of these legends and stories. I would look into the darkness and feel that there were spirits looking back at me, ready and waiting for me to leave the circle of light cast by the candle. I would stay close to my mother or my father. When I went to bed I would hide beneath the blankets so nothing would touch me. Every time I heard a story about something that happened with the Peuchen I would fear them even more. My mind was casting images in the shadows, the Peuchen was always lurking at the edge of the light, never taking a step into it, but always at the edge, ready to stretch a hand and kidnap me. Under my bed I would hear the Leprechauns making a noise, disturbing my sleep as if wanting me to look under the bed so they too could rob me from my parents care. In the daylight when I was playing with the other kids we sometimes heard the whistle of the Salamanca, calling us or anyone of us that would hear it, to its trap. We would run away instantly because we knew the dangers of going to it; or returning its call by form of whistling back at it. I hope right now I'm stirring the fear within you, I hope that right now you feel these stories and become the child that we all are within our hearts; because this is our culture, and we must maintain its life. The day we forget to tell our stories we will disappear, not only our legend but our people also. Today we have called you here to remind you of who we are as a Nation of People! We are going to celebrate our legends and myths. We will have a festival dedicated to Peuchen and all the legendary creatures that are part of who we are and gather to dance, play and understand the importance of our legends. Next week, on the Tuesday night we will gather in full costumes and celebrate Peuchen the most fearsome of our legends, giving it strength and life to go on as our cultural mythology. The dancers will prepare interpretations of the legends to remind us all of some of the characters, and the musicians will play the sounds of the haunting plains. There shall be bonfires and celebration and our guest Ramon, the Shaman that is working with us on the Mapuche Pride will perform some amazing feats of magical display that will top the festivities and bring them to a close. It is important that no matter what happens, no matter what you see, you remain in the arena prepared for the festival. Just like the circle of candle light for as long as you don't get too close to the edge you'll be safe. I am a Mapuche!!!" the Chief raised his right fist as he said the words, and all Mapuche present responded in like manor. The Mapuche were fuelled with new excitement, and left the meeting place talking about different stories they heard when young. The minds of all the Mapuche were dripping life to the world of the Peuchen and she was feeling it. In her own underworld she was happy, it was almost odd for her to feel happy, she was meant to be evil, and somehow that little Shaman was making her soft in the middle. Her creatures were feeling it too, they felt new energy flowing through their veins and they heard the invitation from the children to come and hide under their beds, to poke them whilst they slept tightly under their blankets and to make sounds or blow air in their ears as they slept. The Leprechauns and Duendes ran around the darkness making lustful sounds that were only heard by adults, they were alive with fear from the people of the land.

Ramon was happy with the outcome of the meeting, he was particularly happy with Chief Anibal's speech, the way he addressed the importance of fear and the legends was perfect. He brought back to memory what had been asleep for a long time, that night many children would hear stories from the past and they would sleep perhaps a little lighter however the message was received.

Celeste had sent a message that she would arrive the following weekend; she would be too late for the Peuchen Festival however she was coming soon. Ramon was happy to hear the news. He had organised possible and alternative accommodation near the church and the Chief understood that it was more comfortable for both of them to have some privacy. Everything was falling into place and he felt it was meant to be.

Part seven

Hear the purity of men,
In their sounds and music.
For they know how to tell
A story or legend.

The week went by with many preparations and rehearsals everywhere; The dancers had been practicing and reviving some of the older dances they had not performed in public for decades. The musicians gathered under trees and sat to play their instruments. The sounds of drums, the trutruca and kultrun were new to Ramon's ears, they sounded basic and distorted with a basic rhythm that rose and fell. Chants were accompanying the music and Ramon could see how the dances would fit with it. Finally the night of Tuesday arrived, the Festival preparations were ready for sunset and the piled up wood was ready to be lit into great flames that would cast light far from its pit. People began arriving dressed in colourful costumes, women with long skirts of many layers, blouses and shawls. Necklaces made of silver coins in rows of two, three or four, matching head-dresses with bands of silver coins that allowed others to hang from one central row, ribbons of many colours through their hair and scarfs. Ponchos and wraps over their shoulders, moccasins made from animal hide and drums, lots of drums. The men wore ponchos displaying Mapuche symbols woven by the women of the tribe and mostly a hat or a bandana wrapped around their head, pants and moccasins with a shirt under their ponchos. Their look was that of the Gaucho, the cow herders of the country side and the women the China, or the country women's dress costume. The children were dressed alike, they looked like little dolls in native costumes heavily dressed under layers of material with dirty faces that made them even more beautiful. Smaller fires were all around the camp ready to roast whatever was on the spit, there were some with chicken skewed in twos and threes and others with goats rotated slowly by the hand of the cook. The smell of herbs and spices perfumed the air making ones mouth water in anticipation.

The Machi wore full costume; she presented herself with black vest adorned by silver coins down the front with a black scarf around the head low over her eyes. Silver coins of three rows wrapped around her head like a crown and a row of silver coins hung her head making a chiming sound as she moved. Her drum was bigger, rounder and deep, in a bowl shape, with a stretched hide at the top. Once everyone was settled and before anything else happened she began to chant. Drumming a slow low rhythm and picking up as she chanted at faster speed. As she entered the altered state of the Machi, she began to rock brusquely from side to side, rotating her upper body from side to side. The movement matched the chanting and the drumming sustained all of it together.

Other women joined in with their drums and in seconds it was a concert of beats that imitated mother earth's heartbeat. The Machi chanted word of prayer;

"God up above, listen to us.

Chiefs of antiquity, wise ones listen to the Machi.

I ask for your help, your blessing.

God up above help us, listen to the Machi.

I am the Machi, hence my calling on you.

Oh ancient people come and bring us your power.

Help us, help your Machi.

Let us see today what our legends are to us.

Let the history of the people be part of us.

Oh God and ancient ones, listen to the Machi

And join us. As I go into trance and dance

Bless our people, bless everyone."

The women kept the rhythm as the Machi danced and swayed; they listened to her words and prayed with her in chorus. The energy of the place was opening up, there was a change in ambient pressure and the sky turned orange as the sun touched the horizon. The Machi spun around a few times and stopped her drumming suddenly; the other drums stopped at the same time as if a conductor had signalled for the last note. The unison of spirit was obvious and the Machi danced around the people with leaves and flowers, throwing them at people, brushing them and dusting them with the branches as she danced past them. Then she came to a full stop and pulling her scarf from over her eyes she opened them and smiled. A young woman ran to her with a glass of a drink made from the Monkey Puzzle tree nut, similar to Chicha, fermented seeds that produced a potent alcoholic beverage. The Machi raised her glass and drank it in one gulp.

The celebrations started, a group of dancers came into the centre of the gathering in a step that resembled the Ostrich, holding feathers in their hands making shapes and movements that portrayed a bird with wings; other things hung from their waist. They changed part of the costume as the dance progressed and Ramon realised that the character was Peuchen shapeshifting and he laughed about their interpretation. Dance after dance came and went, the music rose and fell and the chanting's got louder and sometimes was only words accompanied by haunting sounds made by rudimentary instruments; sounds that seemed to embody the open space of the South, the emptiness and desolation that made everything eerie. Women sung native tribal songs that spoke of Maiden's being taken into the forests of long ago. Dances of serpentine nature, duels of monsters, and groups of little people wearing scary masks and chasing what represented little children. The bon fire burned brightly, lighting up the festival camp completely and the sparks rose into a cloudless sky filled with stars that twinkled above the crown of smoke. People were a little drunk with the Chicha, and happy to celebrate their legends. Close to midnight as the number of performances was getting to an end. Ramon dressed in white, his long black hair usually tied back was lose and framed his face; the medallion showing through his open shirt for all to see; took from the bon fire a burning log to set alight a line of fire that would divide the camp into two fields. As the petrol was being poured along the ground he asked for the Chief to make a speech. Chief Anibal, dressed in full costume came forward and stood centred, raising his hands to the sky, the tension of muscles revealed a great physic beneath his poncho, muscular arms and belly that were exposed by the pose he held. The Chief looked like a young warrior that was ready to fight.

"Brothers and sisters of the Mapuche Nation, I stand here proud to be your Chief. For many decades now we have been feeling the weight of oppression creeping in on us. The colonisers encroaching on us pushing us into distant lands and making us feel small and insignificant. Today we celebrate our traditions, our legends and our culture. I'm proud of being a Mapuche Native, I'm proud of our history, past and present. I am proud of our fight for the rights of the people of Patagonia and most of all I am proud of who we are. Today is the beginning of a new era, an era where our legends meet the people that believe in them, that speak of them and fear them. Today is a day where your strength and courage is tested and I urge you to stand with me, to be brave and look at fear in the eye. I am Chief Anibal, Chief of the Mapuche people and I stand with you!" The Chief raised his hands up to the sky again and all the people cheered and applauded. Ramon lit the petrol that had been poured on the grass and a curtain of fire rose from the ground. Then he held his medallion and called Don Ignacio to be present, the old man materialised into a vision for all to see, little frail and wise, his face held a smile of friendliness. Then Ramon called on Don Yuco, who in turn appeared as a projection in the sky; he also smiled at seeing Ramon again after so long. Next Ramon called on Putuma and he too appeared next to Don Yuco, he bowed his head in respect to the Mapuche people. The crowd was astonished, overawed at the visions and a silence fell over the crowd. Ramon spoke to the people with words of wisdom and encouragement.

"People of the Mapuche Nation, these are my teachers and friends, the men who helped me learn about spiritual magic beyond the reality of this world. My teacher and mentor Don Ignacio taught me to be strong and to trust the Great Spirit and its plans for us his instruments. Don Yuco buried me alive to learn to go beyond the body and be free in the world of spirit, and my good friend Putuma helps me when I need guidance and understanding. Today they join us to support the Mapuche face the most important moment of their modern history. Today we celebrate our myths and legends, the things that we fear and have been frightened of for centuries. However they are losing strength and disappearing from our stories; we don't speak of them often enough to give them life, just as our younger Mapuche seek to integrate into the modern society of Argentina to find a place of their own in that society. With it comes a high price, "Forgetting our history and our legends". Today I would like to invite with your permission and support the legends that we still fear. Not to be frightened and run from them but to re-energise them with life as we reenergise our culture and our traditions with renewed pride. Today I invite Peuchen to make herself visible to all and with her, she will bring all the creatures of the Petrified Forest, all of the stories we have been speaking about, especially over the last weeks. I shall now play some magic that will open a portal to the underworld. I ask that you be afraid but not run in fear, for it is important for Peuchen that you still believe in her and all the other creatures in order for them to continue being part of Mapuche culture." Ramon turned to face the curtain of fire and opened his arms to the opposite side of the people. With words that were heard only by Peuchen he called on her to make herself visible to everyone. Don Ignacio and Don Yuco together with Putuma chanted whilst Ramon spoke the words of incantation. The other side of the field started to show signs of a gust of wind swirling the sky around, the people were fixated at what was happening. The light grew into a brightly lit sky and it began streaking as if separating itself into bars of colour, slowly taking the shape of great big trees that rose high into the sky. The leaves shimmered and paths were noticeable through its dense forest; then movement was noticed behind the trees, faces poked out from behind bushes of light, grotesque and horrid. A mass of black that started like a dot in the distance grew in front of Ramon on the other side of the fire wall. Peuchen took shape slowly morphing through a few of her favourite shapes before settling on one that remained for the length of the vision. As Peuchen shapeshifted from form to form; people covered their eyes, children hid under their mother's skirts and behind their fathers. Peuchen laughed loudly creating a mix of lightning storm and magic all in one place. Ramon stood looking intently into her eyes. Peuchen laughed again and looking at Ramon spoke to the Shaman.

"Shaman, nice to see you again! You have brought many friends to this gathering. I see Chief Anibal looking like a great morsel for an afternoon tea. Hahahahhahhha.

Sorry Chief you know my nature, I'm Peuchen I feed on human blood!!!"

"Children!!!" She screamed. The children scurried under tables and skirts as if Peuchen was coming for them.

"Little childreeeeennnnn!!!! Hahahhahahhahhahah" she laughed again.

Ramon knew that Peuchen wanted fear from her people, the ones that gave her life; their fear was making her stronger and bringing more and more creatures out of the forest.

"Peuchen, welcome to our celebration of you, the most feared legend of all Mapuche legends." he said with proud voice.

"Ohhhh my!!!! Shaman you must be careful not to fuel my ego so high, I like that, a Celebration of Peuchen, the most feared legend of the Mapuche!!!" she said with a happy voice.

"It's an honour to be here with all the people that gave life to us and I must say nice to see how many delicious morsels there are among you" she added.

Ramon then spoke on a more serious note. "Peuchen we have celebrated your existence and give life to you through these celebrations, as we do with all the creatures of the underworld. However Peuchen as we spoke on the day you took me on that ride beyond time and space to your world, we face a danger and the danger is of being forgotten, to cease to exist, not only the legends of the Mapuche but also its people. So this celebration is to make sure that the legends go on for generations to come far into the future, to be spoken about with fear, to be remembered and to be wary of all the creatures of the underworld. Do you agree that it's a matter of importance Peuchen?" said Ramon now asking for her to talk.

Peuchen looked at every person there as if she was wetting her appetite. Turning herself inside out and back to a new form she continued.

"I have taken this little Shaman, who refused to be frightened of me! I was mad with rage for his lack of fear. I felt weak, unable to summon enough strange horrors to get a little fear in his eyes. So he spoke wise words that angered me even further but it was only the truth in his words that made me mad! He asked me if I was not afraid of being forgotten. Me!!! Forgotten? Not a chance! However he was right, we have not had many people come by the open space of Patagonia to lure into the underworld. We have not heard our name mentioned much lately and I could see in his eyes that he had no fear. The question he posed to me made me angry because I found truth in it. And it made me realise that if the Mapuche people, my people, those that give life to me forget me, so would they forget their roots, their culture and customs. So Shaman I thank you and most of all I thank the people of this land for celebrating me, the legend of the Mapuche. Peuchen lives and will live forever more in the heart of the future generations, for you little children will speak of the moment when you met Peuchen and the underworld creatures and your children will tell their children and their children will tell their children and so it will go for ever more. I am proud to be a Mapuche legend, the most fearsome of all" and with that she laughed.

The people laughed and cheered as she claimed pride for her linage and applauded as she made a display of her horrific power. For a moment the Mapuche people were not afraid of Peuchen, they were proud of the fearsome legend and they would speak of it for years to come. The Chief stood forward and began chanting, the people joined him, the women began hitting their drums and with the vibration Peuchen and all the underworld creatures became a flood of colour that swirled and exploded into lights of many colours and were sucked into a black hole to leave only stillness and a starry sky for the people to gaze upon. Ramon bowed to Don Ignacio, Don Yuco and Putuma, who even though so far away and some on another dimension, were present. The Machi danced and chanted with the people, the Chief took Ramon by the arm and invited him to dance. The Spirits were high and the mix of fear and exhilaration was deep. Some of the men stayed up all night, drinking Chicha and talking about the legends, their roots and how amazing it was to see them face to face. Sunrise revealed a camp that had been flattened by the people; their feet had stomped and danced to level the field, just like the people had done a long time ago on the top of the mountains that rose to protect those escaping the tsunami. The Mapuche had done it again; their hearts were ignited with pride and belonging, stirred by culture and legend. Ramon saw the sunrise from the veranda, where he drank mate whilst the sun moved ever upwards into the sky. His thoughts were on the festival the night before, his tiredness made it surreal and the magic of it still present in his being. In his sleepy state he heard Don Ignacio speak.

"You are an amazing instrument for the Great Spirits work Ramon! I was so happy to be with you and see our Mapuche brothers celebrate their culture with such Alegria!!! Happiness!!! It took me back to the moments we spent together along the black line, the comradery experienced when the aim is shared as a common purpose by all. The Mapuche will survive as a Nation and they will go on into the future for centuries to come. Our older brothers like us have the strength to face changes and endure them; their children will carry that resilience forward and reinvent their place in the community of modern Argentina, just like we did with the new law reforms in Colombia. People always find a way. May it be by means of faith and prayer or driven by passion and ignorance. It always brings the underdog out of their predicament. I rejoice in seeing the older brother claiming their right all over South America, the time when the Red Way return to walk with man on earth is near and once more the Older Brother shall remain and continue from where they had been interrupted in their journey. God tests his children, only to find out if they respect and fear him. Not because he is a God of Wrath, but because he is an all loving God and wants to see his children remain humble and enjoy the simple and rich life on earth. Man was brought to this land so he could enjoy his existence, procreate and populate this garden. He was given all he needed. Until ego drove men blind and made them become greater than God himself and began to forget his omnipresence. Men lost sight of the greater picture, only seeing the shiny, the pretty and the false wealth they accumulate. The older brother shall rise again to go on and live once more with nature, taking only what he needs and thanking the Great Spirit for the gifts he receives. Ramon we shall remain at your call for when you need us. Thank you for inviting me to be present." Don Ignacio's voice dissipated and Ramon was alone again. Thinking of the old man, he loved so deeply and missed his physical presence, however he was thankful for the access to his spirit form.

Chief Anibal walked onto the veranda, he had slept a few hours and he too was feeling the excitement of the people in his heart and mind. He was elevated by the spirit of his Nation and for once in a long time he felt like a real Chief, he had reached his people and touched their hearts, he represented courage. He sat next to Ramon and began commenting on what people had told him the night before; with pride he recounted some of the words.

"Last night, my people were so happy! Terrified!!! but happy. They said to me that they had not felt so exhilarated in years. Most had not been so scared since they were kids and they even told me that my speech on the meeting night was most touching. It had stirred memories and made them recount them to their children. Last night looking into Peuchens eyes, I felt so strong. I was unafraid of looking into her eyes and become petrified. She made me humble when she said that it was a terrible realisation to have the thought that we could all be forgotten. You told her that! You didn't ask me if I was afraid of being forgotten. But you asked her! And it worked. There is so much truth in that statement, we are the stories we tell, our people know about us because they speak of us and they make us live forever more. We have no written language, we have some stories written but only by the monks that interpreted our stories and wrote them down as they heard them. It doesn't contain the meaning to the Mapuche. It's almost a note on someone's journal, an observation! Our children should write them down, they could be encouraged to interpret them and publish them so our legends, our history and stories are kept from being lost in time. Word of mouth is great in a perfect world; but when you mix the cultures and you have a predominant one the danger becomes greater. Word of mouth is overshadowed by the excess of information and entertainment that comes into your lounge room and grabs your children by their foreheads, steals their mind, their knowledge and they get programed to think they need things they never wanted before.

Ramon, I'm a happy man, I'm glad you accepted our invitation to come and that Jabaro never felt you would not follow him south to us. Thank you" he stretched a hand and held Ramon's forearm, pressed firmly and let go again. Ramon smiled at him, thought for a moment and then he said.

"I never know what I'm going to do when I get asked to help someone. I feel humbled and a sudden responsibility comes over me that drives me to listen to what's shared. Its then that I, like Ceferino, kneel and pray that I may be shown the way to be of help. I, like you, am proud of the response of the people. I have learned so much since I arrived here. My spirit has soared above the plains and the empty land has spoken to me with loud voice. The Mapuche legends have made me confront them without fear. That may be from the lack of knowledge about them or from utter ignorance. One thing for sure is that I know the Great Spirit protects me and guides me. That is what I know Chief. There is plenty of work still ahead of us, let's use this new driving energy to make it happen." Ramon looked at the Chief who had tears in his eyes.

"I have never felt so good about my position as I feel today Ramon, finally I feel I'm a leader for my people, and all of the things I feared doing are renewed by an energy that brings hope to our people. These tears are just that, emotion brought on by happiness, by blessings from the Great Spirit." The Chief got up and walked off. Ramon thought it was time to rest a while. The morning was slow and people were still asleep, perhaps dreaming of Peuchen.

Part Seven

Trust the voice that speaks
Listen with your heart.
For it's there where the truth,
Will speak and trust reside.

Ramon slept for hours, in his dreams he saw Ceferino, who sat at the end of his bed, waiting for Ramon to be aware of his presence in the dream. Ramon saw himself sitting up on the bed. Ceferino was seated sideways, showing Ramon his profile. Ramon studied his face before he spoke. The image of the young Saint reminded him of how early his life had ended. Ceferino spoke about how he had enjoyed seeing his people celebrating the legends. He had felt a lack of connection when he was away from them. The years he spent at school in Buenos Aires had been good and he learned much, but the customs and warmth of his people were a gap he felt greatly.

"When I was sick and my superiors thought that it would be a better idea to take me to Italy to recover in the hills of Turin, then I felt even further away from my people. Italy is a long way from Patagonia. All I had with me were the memories of my culture, the word of my parents in my heart and the devotion to serve God the Almighty. Seeing the children fear the legends last night and the dances that interpreted them was to me like a welcome home. Even though I am free in the world of spirit and have my roots in the nature of God himself, celebrations like these brings back a fondness for my people. Chief Anibal told you that perhaps it would be a good idea to ask the younger generations to write our history down, to interpret the meaning of our legends and stories so they live in the pages of books for ever more. I support that idea. I was expected by my father, the Chief of the Mapuche then, to be the interpreter and secretary to him. I chose to follow the Salesian order instead. My father respected that but I know that in his heart I was his hope for the Mapuche Nation. Our brothers must understand that the world is made of multiple cultures, with belief systems that work perfectly for them. Invasion of lands and pillage is no longer acceptable. Man cannot walk into someone's house and take what he wants because he fancies it. Man must respect other people's ways and their land and realise that there is room on earth for everyone. There are people of pure hearts that offer prayer to me on a daily basis; they pray not for themselves but for the world of men. Those are the rays of sunshine that appear in the dark storm. Those are the people I listen to and grant the miracle they seek; because their hearts are pure, their humbleness is immense and their ego is tamed. Ramon! Fuel the hearts of the Mapuche, take them to Buenos Aires and let the world know the kind of people they are." Ceferino got up and disappeared into the ether. Ramon's eyes opened and he felt blessed for being able to talk to the Saint and his encouragement to pursue his intention to march in the big city.

Ramon spent the next three days organising the new place for Celeste and him. He was now sure that the plan would work, he had the Blessing of Kay-Kay and Saint Ceferino, and the Mapuche people were behind him with great support.

The house was small, a kitchen very simple in nature, a corridor that lead to two rooms with nothing in them other than a wardrobe of some antiquity. Ramon arranged for a bed to be brought to the house, utensils for cooking and a small table and chairs. He washed the walls down to remove the dust that had settled in the empty house and by the Friday night the place was renewed. Celeste would arrive sometime on the Saturday; he wanted her to be comfortable and be able to have space if she wanted to. The Chief had organised a dinner at his place to meet her, as he wanted to know about her and speak about her involvement with their cause.

Ramon took the opportunity of being alone to sit down and call in on Brava, it had been weeks and he missed her. He had not been able to drive to a town with a library and access to the internet. He had no idea what was happening with Saraphina and how things had gone when she returned to Melbourne. He held the medallion and thought of Brava, Gato and Atticus, soon his mind's eye was beginning to perceive their silhouettes in the jungle. Gato was the first one to feel his presence, the cat had been resting on the log near Brava's hut as Ramon began finding his form appearing at the camp. Gato jumped down from the log and ran to rub his face on Ramon's hands.

"Gato how are you!!! spoke Ramon as he rubbed his chin and caressed his ears.

"Good Ramon, happy to see you! How are you doing? said the cat with his thoughts.

"Good, very good, we are making progress. I need to speak to Brava about things, I miss you big boy" spoke Ramon to the cat and kissed him on the head.

"She is inside", said the cat and followed Ramon to Brava's hut.

"Brava, hija!" "Brava, my daughter! called Ramon.

Brava, was writing some notes in her journal and she heard something calling her, low in the distance. She felt her father's energy and she held the tooth necklace just to make sure. As she did she heard his voice clearly and ran out the door.

"Dad!!! You are back, great to see you. I missed you. How are you?" she asked excitedly.

"Great darling, so much has happened since I saw you last. There is much happening and I think you could help me out. I'm thinking of organising a march for the Mapuche brothers, but I think that if we take it to a continental level it would serve as a bigger impact worldwide." said Ramon.

"Ok, so how can I help with it?" asked Brava.

"I would like to organise that every country and its native people in Latin America do the same as we are doing on the same day at the same time. I would like to involve the TV Networks and get it televised all over the world. Could you mobilise the people in Peru and neighbouring countries. I shall ask Don Yuco to join us in spreading the word through the northern countries right up to Mexico with the Aztec and Maya descendants." said Ramon.

"WOW!!!" Responded Brava, "That's my Dad, don't do anything small" she laughed. "Yes Dad, can you give me details, purpose and dates so that we can fine tune the preparations to join your cause. I was getting a little worried I was never going to work with you on anything important again. But Voila! Here it is." She was happy to be asked.

"Great my dear, I have little time now; I shall write soon with details please keep an eye out for it. Give me a few days. I love you Brava, how is Atticus?" he asked as an afterthought.

"He is fine, he speak Spanish really well now and is attending school with the Kakataivo kids. He is growing very fast." Brava smiled.

"Have you had news from Saraphina?" asked Ramon.

"Yes, she is sounding strong, apparently she has finished with her partner Mykha, I think things went a bit askew and she didn't like what he had been doing all along. She has been asking after you. Can you get a message to her?" asked Brava.

"If you speak to her before I have a chance, tell her to wear her jaguar tooth necklace so we can all communicate in this manner. I have no easy access to computers or power. It would be better to do it this way now that we can". suggested Ramon.

"Ok Dad, I shall. I love you and miss you. Oh by the way Atticus told me to tell you that he loves you to infinity and beyond double infinity times." she laughed and so did Ramon.

"Give him my love and tell him I'll be back before school finishes."

Ok, Dad, take care." Brava stood with Gato beside her. The cat looked at Ramon and blinked a good bye. Ramon disappeared into the ether and the sounds of the desert were present in his ears once again.

The Machi had been looking into the bowl, she poured the oil droplets into the dish and watched the drops form, come together or disperse. In her state of contemplation she saw Celeste; tall and slender, cascading long blond hair that gave her the appearance of a mermaid. The Machi saw Celeste's hands moving fast through keyboards and interpreted the vision as the hands of someone intelligent, someone who knows. She saw Celeste among people, trading, selling and gave her the impression that the woman was well connected. The Machi sat back on the chair and looked into the distance; she also was now expecting Celeste's arrival to the town.

Saturday began with commotion; a herd of cows had got lose and ran out on to the road causing a stir in the town. The farming traffic of the morning was a chaotic mess that blocked the one street that traversed the town. Ramon laughed about the incident and the way local people dealt with it. The cows refused to move and the herders were trying to push the cows from their behinds to get them off the road; a futile effort from little short men not strong enough to move the great animals. Eventually things cleared and Ramon went in search of staple foods, like bread, butter and jams. The Machi saw him walk by and offered eggs, half a loaf of homemade bread and tomatoes. Ramon accepted the items with pleasure all he needed now was fresh milk. Inside his heart he was excited about seeing Celeste, his visit to Buenos Aires had given them an opportunity to spend some time together and that only made them realise how much they had missed out on. She would soon be with him again and that would make his heart glad.

Celeste arrived at three thirty five pm. Ramon saw the dust raised by her car far down the road and a smile formed on his lips. Celeste drove slowly through the street until she saw him step onto the road to signal her of where to stop. She stepped out of the car into an embrace that confirmed his gladness to see her. People quickly gathered around them welcoming her and introducing themselves as who they were. Celeste smiled and kissed some of them in the Argentinian custom of greeting. Chief Anibal came out of the house and walked up to them.

"Now Ramon, you have kept secrets from me. She is a beautiful woman and a Shaman should be careful of his heart being lost to such beauty! The Chief smiled and embraced Celeste, she felt instantly welcome by Chief Anibal, who stole her from Ramon and led her to the veranda of his house.

The cook promptly brought fresh water with lemon to the table, homemade bread and a selection of cheese and cold meats, olives and red wine. The Chief asked Celeste what she would like to start with and Celeste responded that she would like a glass of wine and a moment to run into the toilet as the drive had been long and her bladder was full. Everybody laughed and the cook showed her the way to the toilet. Ramon laughed as he looked at Chief.

"You are a flirt" he said to the Chief.

"You kept that a secret didn't you? She is beautiful!!! What a woman!" said the Chief as he slapped Ramon on the back in approval. Ramon smiled again and winked an eye to the Chief, "you'll see, she is my special one"

Celeste was back and sat to enjoy the refreshments; she took a sip of wine and commented on the fruitiness of its taste. The Chief told her how sorry he was that she could not have been there a few days earlier. The celebration of Peuchen was an amazing experience had by all. Celeste looked at Ramon and made a comment about being filled in on the detail of it later. Ramon smiled and nodded. The Chief and all gathered were eager to hear what Celeste was able to bring into the cause. Celeste responded that she was only an instrument for Ramon's instructions. That she would do whatever was necessary for the cause at hand and that she had experience with the world of the internet and was good at setting petitions up and distributing information as required. "I'm here, eager to be part of it" she said.

Her hands had trouble not to reach out and touch Ramon, he had sat next to her and her feet were now entwined in his, below the table and away from view. There was an exchange that spoke of how much she missed him.

The Machi arrived and with eyes that looked deep into the soul she approached Celeste. Ramon looked at her and raised an eyebrow inferring for her to stop reading Celeste's thoughts. This is the Machi, the medicine woman of the tribe" Celeste stood up and made a gesture to hug the Machi but felt it was inappropriate to do so and instead shook her hand. The Machi held Celeste's hand with both of hers; smiling and looking deep into the woman's eyes she kissed her on the cheek.

"Welcome, Bien venida Celeste a nuestra tierra!. Welcome to our land Celeste!

The Machi was shown a chair and she took her space making herself comfortable, she sat across from Celeste and watched her constantly. Ramon watched the Machi. The Chief spoke jovially about the fuelled hearts of the Mapuche and the plans for the future. He told Celeste that the Gods had blessed them and their Saint, San Ceferino had also given his blessing. Celeste smiled and rejoiced at the news. "Looks like you guys have been busy here. That's great!" she added. Celeste was feeling a little uncomfortable by the look of the Machi, she was too intense and Celeste had no escape from her eyes. Ramon told Celeste about how the Machi was good at readings and that perhaps while she was among them she could have a reading from the Machi and see what she had to tell. The Machi was happy to hear Ramon's reference to her; she would be interested in seeing into Celeste's life and know more about the woman that seemed to be from another reality. The hours passed by and the wine got to some of the guests head, turning stories into sobs and serious incidents into laughter. Ramon felt it was time to leave the gathering and claim some space alone with Celeste. The Machi had departed at sunset, returning home to feed her cats; however most of the people remained with the Chief. As they left the veranda the Chief made a joke about noise levels and how in the open country things can be heard far away! Everybody laughed and clapped at his joke. Ramon picked up an apple and showed them all. "You know what I'm going to do with this apple, don't you? There will be no sound" he laughed and Celeste smacked him jokingly.

At the house after dropping her travel bag on the bed they entwined in a frenzy of kisses. Soon they were both naked and Ramon kneeled to the ground and kissed her soft belly. He rubbed his face on her silky skin and with gentle kisses murmured how much he had missed her. At hearing his words Celeste pulled him up to her lips and kissed him again. The candle went out and they lay on the bed, allowing their bodies to be rediscovered. Her mane of hair covered his chest, entangled itself in every kiss and tied them to each other. She sat up on his loins and gathered her hair into a bun fastened by a knot of some strands around it. Ramon looked at her breasts that hung heavily with aroused nipples. He kissed them and spoke words of pleasure at kissing them. She sighed and wanted to feel him deep inside her; he obeyed and penetrated her as deep as he could. The night passed and morning found them embraced in each other's arms. The bed a mess of linen that showed vigorous activity as proof of their encounter.

After breakfast Ramon took her for a walk along the dusty road, before the sun got too hot to be out there in the open. He spoke about the legends and how they lure victims that wander away from others. He warned her about not going too far alone and if she heard a whistle whilst out there not to respond as that is the Salamanca, trying to get a response from anyone that would hear it. "If you respond by whistling back, the Salamanca will appear and try to make a deal with you. It has the power of suggestion and it will make you think that there are things you want and it will make you trade your soul for it." Ramon was serious about the warning. Celeste frowned and promised to be safe.

"So tell me about what has happened since I last saw you?" she asked.

"So much has happened; I have learned so much about these people, their culture, their ways and their incredible legends. I have had so many visions, I've been kidnaped by the most fearsome of all legends and I shall not mention her name so that you don't call her mentally" Ramon spat words out as if he was ranting and raving. Celeste looked at him and laughed out loud.

"Wow!!! Ok, looks like you have had some experiences but I'm not so familiar with all of them so slow down a bit." She said kissing his lips and looking at him like she wanted him again. Ramon looked around and saw the valley devoid of people. He walked off the road and took a turn toward a river that crossed the desolate land a few hundred meters away from the dusty road. The river was a narrow line of water that ran from hills far from where they stood, however the water was clear and the rock pools that formed at its bank were refreshing. Ramon took Celeste's shirt off, he kissed her breast and undressed himself and she finished kicking her pants off and pushed them to one side. Standing naked in the open country and only kissed by the sun's rays they felt aroused and free. Ramon was erect and she looked at his penis with desire. This time she went on her knees and kissed him around his loins and engulfed his penis with her mouth; he closed his eyes in pleasure and feeling he was close to orgasm pulled out of her mouth before it was too late. He lay next to her and feeling the stones warmth on his skin asked her to mount him. She followed instruction and rode his body to ecstasy, both reaching orgasm and screaming free in the open air. After a while of resting close to one another, they washed in the river pools, the fresh water making the raw skin burn reminding them of their sexual activity.

On their way back to the house Ramon told her of the plan to organise a march through the centre of Buenos Aires, finishing up on Plaza de mayo, the square outside the Government House. A peaceful march, with banners stating the "Mapuche Pride, National Pride," It's to mark the tenth anniversary of Saint Ceferino's beatification. The Saint is the Mapuche Pride and our National Pride.

"What do you think?" he asked.

"I think it's a great idea. The truth is that the Mapuche have been standing for their right for decades, they turn up protesting every so often but nothing seems to move forward for them. This is perhaps the best way to show the people of Argentina that they are the true Argentinians and they have given the people of this country a Saint!" she stated.

"Not just a Saint, the only South American indigenous Saint in the Catholic Church!!!" finished Ramon with a smile.

"A Mapuche Saint!!! That is a great way to show it to the world! The people of Argentina love him very much, they will all join in on the march and it would make it safer for the Mapuche to be marching the streets" Celeste added.

"So what do you need me to start organising" asked Celeste.

"When we get back to the house we shall meet with the Chief and we'll talk about the planning of the March of the Mapuche Pride" he said, "but for now let's walk in the silence of the valley."

Ramon and Celeste walked in silence holding hands, looking into the vastness of the country side; every now and then they would speak of the letters he had sent her every Tuesday for the last five years. Ramon told her that it was the way he could be with her no matter what the world required of him.

"I write these letters to inspire you, to meet you mentally and excite you intelligently. A person can have lovers, or make love all he or she wants. But to be elevated by the belief that there is a person, one who every day thinks of you, asks nothing of you and gives to you words that paint images in your mind, a person that makes you feel close and that you can breathe them in with every word is a much better compliment. More than having all the lovers in the world. I write to you because I want you to find strength in your day, to go through whatever presents itself to you, the highs and the lows. I want my words to be the sunshine when it's raining outside, the warmth of the fire when it's cold. Company when you feel alone and quiet when there is too much noise. I can't give you more than that. I cannot commit to be with you as your husband when the world needs me. To put you through my absence whilst being your partner would be too much to ask of anyone. The situation would change and would make you feel I have no time for you in my life and instead of being inspirational to you I would be the man who leaves you behind alone. Does that make sense to you?" asked Ramon.

"Sometimes I wish I could follow you wherever you go, to be beside you and never lose sight of you. Be your accomplice in everything you do, good or bad!!!" she smiled at him.

"But at the same time I don't want to leave my family, all that I have achieved and the people that I love. Perhaps it's on the Sunday nights when it's close to Tuesday and I anticipate the arrival of your letters that I feel most vulnerable. I know that what you have done in Colombia and in Peru would have been a challenge for me to endure, and I don't know if I could leave everything, every comfort and commit to a cause like you do. I understand that the cause or each cause requires something different from you. Looking around here for example, I know that these three days are a little holiday with you Ramon for me; and its fine and refreshing but the thought of being here, living here for months on end in the middle of nowhere where the nothingness screams so loud, would drive me crazy!." Celeste laughed with him.

"It's Ok, we have an understanding that not many would be happy with, but it works for us. I'm free to do what I want and so are you and as long as you keep in touch and you ask me to be part of your crusades I shall be happy." Celeste kissed him again, stopping their walk to make sure he got all of her mouth and embrace. Then looking at him as if he had stolen a kiss from her without permission, she smiled and continued on.

Dinner with the Chief was always entertaining and after the usual flirting the conversation took a serious note. The Chief asked Ramon of the plans for the March and Ramon began to tell them what he had thought and how it should be organised.

"Well, the date is on the eleventh day of the eleventh month twenty seventeen. So I want you to pay attention to these numbers. If you look at them as numbers you can see that we have the numbers 11 repeating themselves twice, however when you add up 2017 together as one number it becomes one. 20 plus 17 is 37 and 3 plus 7 is 10 then one plus zero is one. So we have the number 1 five times, 11 day, 11 month with the number one added from the year. 5 ones! That is a highly psychic number. Not only that but the western countries celebrate remembrance day on that day giving us two more number ones, because the time they celebrate and hold a minutes silence in memory of all who fell in battle is at 11 am, making that seven ones; the number of the highest vibration in the spiritual plan". Ramon stopped for a minute to release his excitement. So see it written down so you can understand it." Said Ramon as he reached for a piece of paper and began writing the numbers down.

11 day, 11 month, 11 hour, plus 1 for the sum of the year = 7 ones

"The one minute silence held in respect of the fallen soldiers gives us the extra number 1 to be used as the resonance with their hearts and sorrow. The moment we appeal to the world for our freedom and native rights. San Ceferino gave us that blessing long ago, the universe and the Gods have planned this a long time before we became too tired of the oppression and disadvantage experienced by our people and what has been done to them by the colonists. The Saint is blessing us with his presence and marching with us!" The chief and Celeste studied the numbers.

"I have not mentioned this before, but because it's the five hundred and twenty fifth anniversary of colonisation I believe it a great idea to rise even higher and ask the native tribes of Latin America to join us in their respective countries. If all the indigenous people of Latin America that are experiencing the same fate rise with us, the world will be shaken and a new understanding shall emerge. Today when you listen to the news our brothers in the United States are fighting for their land rights, and access to clean water. The Dakota people have been standing strong to stop oil pipes crossing and poisoning their rivers. The American President is a clown that even though blind and bigoted is fuelling people all-over the world to stand for antidiscrimination and harassment of Native lands and titles. The people of Mexico are rising to fight for their rights to stay as citizens of the United States and those that have remained in Mexico are protesting against his stupidity and insults. The world all over is standing up. Women march in protest against abuse and for equal opportunity. They stand for their intelligence and not as mere sexualised objects for man's entertainment. The people of South American countries have done combined marches before, I remember travelling through Peru, Salvador and Colombia and the United States in nineteen ninety two, the year marking five hundred years of Colonisation. The people of the land stood, celebrated and stated their rights, culture and made public appeals to the world about their oppression." Ramon brought a fist down on the table that enwrapped the power of what he was saying.

"I think that we could do the same thing today, this year. I believe that we can organise for an emissary of the U.N. to be present and submit publically in front of everyone in Argentina an enquiry into Native Titles and Native Rights. And you Chief Anibal will be the Chief that announces that in front of the Government House in Plaza de Mayo. The Mapuche Chief stands with his people and the world and demands to be heard. Celeste, I need you to start investigating the process for a submission to the U.N on Indigenous rights, Indigenous Land Rights and Indigenous Titles and applications for autonomy and economic growth. Also obtain the necessary paperwork to organise that and find out if we can have a representative of the U.N to be present on the day of the March. Let's do whatever needs to be done." Ramon continued with instructions and delegation.

"Any specialist applications should be sent to Makkah, she will write the application and submit it. She helped us with the Mamo in Colombia and did a fantastic job of it. Celeste you need to stay in touch with her, just like you did before, you feed all information necessary to the appropriate people. Also investigate what we need to know about applications, what proof they desire us to include. I also need you to contact every Cardinal or Archbishop in Buenos Aires for the day of celebrating San Ceferino anniversary. If we can organise a news feed or group email to include all the churches in the country we should do that. Do you think we can obtain an address book of all the churches in the country?" he asked Celeste.

"I'm sure I can organise something! Leave it with me." she replied.

"Chief Anibal, I want to know what affiliation or representation the Mapuche have or have had from organisations that have fought for these rights previously. If you could supply us with details that would be great. I would like you to take care of speaking to the Mapuche people in Chile and ask them to rise with us on the day and claim their rights also. If I leave it to you can you keep me informed on how far you have moved with it and what responses you get! Remember that everything is important, any little thing, a word you hear or a comment that is made is important, we cannot disregard anything at all for it can be what brings our effort undone. I need you to keep Brava posted, she is talking to friends in Ecuador, Salvador and Brazil apart from the people of Peru, she will be mobilising the march over there. Don Yuco will speak to the people of Colombia and Venezuela all the way up to Mexico. We should waste no time as when we think about it its only seven months before the date." Ramon turned from Chief Anibal and asked.

"Celeste can we drive to the nearest town to have access to Wi-Fi? I need to get some stuff done and send messages to my friends over the internet. Also I would like to check my emails and write to my daughters." said Ramon.

"Yes I'd love to, tomorrow morning?" suggested Celeste.

"Yes please its only one more day before you return to Buenos Aires and I need to do this soon, so we can be clear with everyone and what they will be doing." They both agree to an early start. Ramon was fuelled with drive and excitement, Celeste was aroused at seeing the way Ramon worked live!!! She had only worked with him through the internet before. The Chief was dizzy and admired Ramon's mind and the diligence he showed at organising people. He was happy to be there with him more than any other he could choose. No wonder the brothers of Colombia and Peru had called on him.

Part Eight

In the distance that separates us
Our hearts unite,
For we stand strong as brothers, sisters
One human kind.

Celeste and Ramon drove out to the nearest town early the next morning; they decided they would have breakfast in the town. There was a small library that had WIFI and Celeste had brought her laptop with her. Ramon logged in to his emails and discovered that there were three hundred and seventy six emails waiting to be read. He skimmed through looking for the ones from his daughters. All others were less important at that minute. He saw one from Brava, where she told him how much she missed him and how things were getting busier at La Cintura Research Station. He skimmed the rest of the email to make sure he wasn't missing anything important; however he already had spoken to Brava about it in one of his astral visits. Searching through the rest of the emails he found one from Saraphina, she had sent it weeks prior, not long after they parted company in Peru. The email addressed what was happening back at home in a brief manor, she had stated how happy she was about what she had learnt in Peru and how she enjoyed being with the family there. That she missed Atticus dearly but was happy that he stayed to learn and grow with issues of importance for his future and the future of the world he would be involved with in his adulthood. She stated that "Things with Mykah were as they should be. She had taken care of it and she was back in Ramon's house. Don't worry about your plants; they'll be watered now that I'm here." With it a smiley face emoji.

Ramon thought for a moment; he knew that she was stronger after the awakening of her memories in the Ayahuasca ceremony. However he worried about Mykah, he had known much more than he ever wanted Saraphina to realise and now obviously she had confronted him about it all. Things seemed to have gone alright since she had returned home. He would have to have a talk with her about it.

Brava had sent one more email, in its message she had stated that the volunteer numbers had tripled over the last few weeks and they were thinking of buying more land to join the Kakataivo land and also accommodate the increased demand for placements from all over the world. It was at reading these words that Ramon had an idea.

He sat to write a reply to Brava with instruction for the march on the eleventh day of the eleventh month of the year twenty seventeen at eleven am. "We will be marching along the city centre from the Congress Plaza to Plaza de Mayo finishing up at Government House; where Chief Anibal will make a speech and present our submission to the U.N. for a human rights, land rights and Native rights investigation on the Argentinian Government." He said. "If you can organise that all neighbouring countries around Peru march and deliver their message at the same time in their respective capital cities; that will have a world impact. The people must rise and claim their rights. Say no more, enough is enough! Reading your emails, I realised that you have access to the support of your volunteers, would you please ask them to send messages to all their friends everywhere in the world and ask for support. Petitions work well, signatures, they can sign petitions and we can present the results to the U.N. as support for investigations all over South America. They will have their work cut out for them." he continued.

"Brava remember that it's about thinking laterally, the more use of contacts we can make, the faster the word will spread. Can you also send message to Caro and Alana and also Pinky in Melbourne, the universities alone will amount to thousands of signatures and will feel included fuelling their participation in our cause once more.

I love you, take care of yourself and be careful."

Dad, Ramon.xoxo

As soon as he had finished the email to Brava he wrote a quick message to Saraphina, telling her that because of the lack of access to computers and power he preferred if she could wear her tooth necklace so they could talk remotely.

'I asked Brava to let you know a few days ago, this is my first chance of accessing my emails. So I hope you are doing alright and that everything is calm at your end. I shall call on you through meditation for a talk.

 Love Dad, Ramon xoxo'

He continued on with messages to many people in his address book. Makkah in Persia, Anis and Melina in the Netherlands, John from Mississippi, and David Jacques in France, Jan in Scotland and a reinforcement message to Pinky and Alba Luz in Australia. They had been instrumental in helping out with the Colombian issue and had raised millions of signatures in a matter of weeks, they would assist once again as they were still involved in the Colombian law reforms watchdog campaign.

Dear friends,

Once again I approach you with a request for support. This time the native people of Argentina, the Mapuche. They have suffered countless humiliations and discrimination on the grounds of their origin. Being a native Mapuche is not cool in today's world. So their opportunities, their rights to be and their rights to any participation in society are reduced to minimal acceptance. These are five hundred year old issues my friends and I cannot stand beside them and watch what society inflicts upon them. The Mapuche are a kind ancient people. Strong and proud of their roots, their native lineage and most of all their culture. We are mobilising the whole of South America to stand for their rights. All native nations will march in their respective capital cities and claim their rights to be, to remain and to be free from discrimination and oppression. Would you join us once again and support us and the Native societies of these countries to stand and be counted in a democratic society. I will post and send short films of their celebrations for public viewing and support of your organised petitions. Please, the collection of signatures and distribution of awareness all over the world is what I ask of you.

Always with you.

Ramon.

Ramon uploaded a short video of the Mapuche Machi singing and dancing in a medicinal healing with the people gathered around her in traditional costumes. He attached it to the email and forwarded it to all on the list.

Celeste had been on her phone gathering information they could use, checking some of the human rights and native title acts when she came across something of interest. She showed Ramon and asked if it was what they needed. Ramon read it.

'Indigenous communities, peoples and nations are those which, having a historical continuity with pre-invasion and pre-colonial societies that developed on their territories, considered themselves distinct from other sectors of the societies now prevailing in those territories, or parts of them. They form at present non-dominant sectors of society and are determined to preserve, develop and transmit to future generations their ancestral territories, and their ethnic identity, as the base of their continued existence as peoples, in accordance with their own cultural patterns, social institutions and legal systems.

(United Nations, "Study of the Problem of Discrimination against Indigenous Populations," (New York: UN Sub-Commission on the Prevention of Discrimination and Protection of Minorities, 1986). UN Document E/En.4/Sub.2/1986/7Add.4, Paragraph 379.)

Ramon smiled and kissed her," You are so good, this is enough for us to submit our petition, there will be more that will turn up but I'm happy with this already!"

Celeste kissed him back and said, "You know it and don't forget it!"

Ramon was very happy and so was Celeste, even though she was to return to Buenos Aires the next morning, she was happy to be with him in that very moment.

They spent a few hours in the town alone, sitting at a restaurant, eating lunch and discussing other details. Ramon told her that the Salesian monks would get in touch with all their networks throughout Argentina, however they should make sure that the Catholic Churches were contacted also and joined in on the celebration of Saint Ceferino. Celeste took some notes and then closed the notebook. She held his hand and asked him if they could walk.

"Can we have a little window shopping? I want to walk and hold your hand without thinking about the world's problems for a moment." she said looking at his eyes with love.

"Yes of course we can. The world is in need of fast action though, it's all well and good to want to have a little mind space but it's imperative that we don't lose momentum." Ramon spoke as if looking ahead of time in his mind. They left the restaurant and walked out to the quiet street, where there were a few shops that sold souvenirs and crafts from local artisans. They frolicked through the items and Celeste chose one that she liked. She wanted to have something that reminded her of that day. Ramon took it in his hand and looked at it. "Recuerdo de La Pampa, Souvenir from La Pampa" he smiled and suggested she should take a mate gourd as a souvenir instead of the little barometer. She replied that it would sit on her wall and she would see it all the time and remind her of that very morning.

Back at the Chief's house things were getting busy, the chief had looked for paperwork that would show him previous attempts to law reforms, old applications and the organisations that had supported them. There was the Mapuche Indigenous Centre, Mapuche Advocacy Agencies and the Mapuche Indian legacy of Argentina Society that had made application for law reforms and land titles and the inclusion of economic development of the Land and territories of Native tribes in Argentina. They had been dismissed or lost in the political turmoil or the political upheaval of the country, every time they proceeded with an application something would happen in the political arena and the paperwork would get lost or the previous government was blamed for it. It was impossible to move forward with anything in such a poor state of accountability by any agency or government department. Chief Anibal kept the paperwork for Ramon; he had kept every piece of paper ever submitted to the government and had some that went back before his time as a Chief.

That night when Ramon and Celeste returned and joined the Chief for dinner they discussed what each of them had found as support for their application. Ramon read the paragraph from the U.N. website and told the Chief that they had enough in that paragraph to support and lodge an application.

"There would be more uncovered and Celeste will procure it and get back to us," said Ramon.

Chief Anibal brought the folder with all copies of previous applications to show both of them. They went through and read dates, outcomes and applications relevant to the days situation.

"Ok, looks like we have to start all over again, nothing came of these ones and we cannot go through it again. If the government does not take responsibility for their departments and everything gets lost and dismissed, then the march is what needs to happen next. We can back up our application with these copies of all previous ones and ask the U.N. to investigate why each and every one of them got lost in the system." Ramon was feeling frustrated with the Argentinian government and the way they just removed what they didn't want to be bothered with out of sight, one could never win. They would stretch any process out until one would give up or was broke from spending money on legal advice and representation. Ramon was not going to go through that again. Makkah will follow our application through until they give us an answer. If our friends from all over the world send us support signatures from the website campaigns, that will support our application and when they see on TV that the whole of Latin America is uprising for their rights and that we all support each other; now!! that will expose everyone that has never responded or done anything about our submissions before and the investigation will make them responsible for their lack of responsibility. It could well work to our benefit. The U.N. will see how long the Mapuche have tried to be heard by the government and it will sanction the government of Argentina for not being responsible in the exercise of Human Rights and Indigenous Titles;" concluded Ramon.

Chief Anibal smiled, "May the Gods hear you Ramon! And I believe that this time we march, no more chances to be ignored or pushed back!"

"That's the way a Chief speaks!" said Celeste as she held his hand in support.

The night had come and the clock marked eleven thirty five pm, it was late and it had been a long day. Ramon and Celeste left the Chiefs house and walked to their place a few hundred meters away. The night was clear; stars twinkled brightly in the sky and Celeste stopped to look at them and take their twinkling in to her heart. It had been a long time since she had seen a sky that bright and it made it special that she was holding his hand under such a beautiful display of light.

"Do you know what I used to think stars were when I was a kid?" asked Ramon to Celeste.

"No, tell me" she replied hugging him closer.

"I used to think that stars were little holes in the ceiling of earth that let the light of heaven through and that's how we knew where heaven was, it was on the other side of the dark sky of night," he smiled and added, "Innocence is such a blessing, isn't it?"

"Yes, it certainly makes everything much more pure!" replied Celeste as they walked on.

That night they lost themselves in gentle caresses and all the kisses they had missed out over the years, making love and speaking the words their hearts wanted to hear; words that were necessary to feed their relationship. Ramon promised that he would soon visit her in Buenos Aires to continue where they left off. Celeste was to keep in touch with him as often as she needed to. He was going to get transport to the town for internet access every three days, to keep up with the necessary information and progress that was fed to him by her regarding contacts and web results. Next morning she left after breakfast; Nora, the Machi had joined them and the Chief had given her a present, as a token of his admiration. The feather of an eagle entwined with leather and cotton strings for her to hang on her rear vision mirror.

"It will keep you safe", he had said as he gave it to her with an embrace that showed he was fond of Celeste.

Ramon embraced her outside by the car and after exchanging a few words she drove off back to the big city. The Chief came over to Ramon and putting his arm around him said in a soft voice as if he was telling a secret.

"I bet you are going to miss her" then shook him as if to wake him out of a dream.

Part Nine

Tell me your dreams
For they reveal your heart's desire,
Tell me your goals
For they wait on the mountain's summit.

Ramon spoke to the Chief asking how the Mapuche people took to the beatification of Ceferino, did they find any division among their people, did the Mapuche brothers from Chile support it and were they happy for the Argentinian Mapuche? He was trying to gather a little understanding of how a nation of aborigines react to the white man's religion and imposition of their religious beliefs on the native people. The Chief responded, thinking for a moment then gaining composure and memories he began.

"There were approximately sixty thousand people that attended the beatification; it was a great thing to witness. There were Mapuche and European together celebrating the Saint. Flags, both Mapuche and Catholic blew in the wind as if a multi-coloured serpentine was thrown into the air. Chimpay was filled to the brim with visitors; people from neighbouring countries had come to witness the beatification ceremony. Chile brothers with their flags and Bolivian brothers, Uruguay, Paraguay even some people from Peru and Brazil. I was very proud. Ceferino's family were there, they were honoured with the blessing of Ceferino.

Officials from the Vatican, like the Pope; Archbishops and Cardinals, and the Vice President came to Chimpay to officiate at the ceremony. It was presented as a multicultural event. It was implied that Ceferino was the bridge that connected the church and the native tribes; the one that finally united the two together. It was a great day for the general Mapuche community. There were some that refused to attend. They believed that the Church was using Ceferino as a band aid, something to repair what they had done to the native people over hundreds of years. They stated that they did not accept such evil title for a brother who died at the hands of colonization itself. Other members of the Mapuche Education Centre considered that he belonged to this land and they thought it was outrageous that he is still being used to dominate and Christianise our people as if our ways were wrong and we are heathen. They felt that native people like the Mapuche were not allowed to practice their belief systems as the Christian Church didn't believe in their Gods, hence the push for educating the native people of Latin America in Christian beliefs. They were outraged!" said the Chief.

"Would you say that most Mapuche people are happy to have Ceferino seen as a Saint all over the world. Is the general consensus of the native people an elevated one toward the event?" asked Ramon.

"We are in a predicament!" the Chief replied. "On one hand we want to remain independent and preserve our ways and culture; on the other we need to assimilate and integrate with the modern society of today in order to go on living. We educate our children in the colonisers system so we can learn to deal with them effectively. Five hundred years have passed and the white man is not learning our ways, and are not interested in our language or systems of governance. They take advantage of the haphazard way we try to achieve things. In a world that communicates through media of all sorts we can no longer remain non participant. The President of Bolivia made an announcement promising all people of Bolivia access to the internet, no matter what socioeconomic group they belonged to, or what roots they had. When you think that the world today has a hand in everything, and they can reach through a device from the other side of the world and either help or harm you; you've got to consider how you are going to survive what the world is coming to. No longer are we isolated if that is your fear. We may be isolated geographically but when it comes to communication we can reach out far if we want to. Our younger generations are being swallowed by computers; they are awakening to a bigger world. We join them or we disconnect completely. As you've said to Peuchen about being forgotten. We have no written language of our own and if we don't make the effort to preserve our history, our legends and our ways will disappear even though there may be Mapuche people that remain. This new way of communicating can be our salvation. We cannot pretend that our language will survive, when everybody today speaks English as the communication language of the internet. Over the years I have noticed how the Castilian spoken in this country has changed because of the internet. New words, new terms that were never in existence before, now they're accepted as current language. That is what I mean. We have to make amends and fight the situation we face with modern skill and then we may have a chance. The Mapuche people are known for their warrior courage; however I'm afraid that today strength is not what can win a battle. Intelligence is." The Chief looked at Ramon with understanding. He was right, the people of his Nation couldn't survive the rudimentary way they lived in a world that moved so fast. People today are informed by the screen they carry in front of their eyes twenty four seven. Statistic results show that humanity is sleep deprived, because of the need to see, read and respond to any stupid message at any time of the night, as if the awareness of it could show one to be less up to date than with the IN thing. Other statistical results show that children spend less than thirty percent of their time outdoors per week; this is direct proof of the new world addiction to the small screen. The people at the top have devised great ways to make sure humanity does not see anything around them. The way consumerist psychology works makes humans addicted to anything new. Most people only care about their comfort, never mind about what's happening out there.

Ramon thought for a moment about the Chiefs words. He then spoke about why he wanted to raise awareness through the internet; he noticed that the Chief had good understanding of the effects of this type of communication.

"I'm glad you spoke in that way! You have given me an understanding of how much you know about cyber space and how you can use it. We are raising awareness about our situation here through such medium and that will be the way we can make some changes. There are people all over the world that care, are genuinely interested in human rights and the predicament of others. I have said it before; people from western cultures have the means to help. Their lives are or can be devoid of meaning and helping others is what they need in order to fulfil their lives as better humans. I know many people who actively support causes and send donations to whatever cause there may be. They have power, their power is to help and support and that is what we are going to harvest, their support." Ramon stopped and thought for a moment more. The Chief smiled at him and said.

"Well-spoken Ramon"

Ramon looked at the Chief and locked in his eyes, he asked.

"Chief do you know what seems to be the biggest problem in western societies?"

The Chief thought for a few seconds and then nodded as negative.

"No, not really."

"Western societies have one battle of their own." Ramon replied. "There is an epidemic of depression, induced by processed foods, chemicals and preservatives. These people are a burden to society; the money spent in supporting them costs billions to some countries. The other is teen-age depression; they cut themselves as if it's going out of fashion. Mutilating, they say they do it because they can't feel anything, cutting themselves releases some pain and it makes them feel. Then there is an epidemic of drugs, this affects two groups of people; in their early twenties and early forties. Their families are destroyed by the effects these drugs have on the subject that consumes them. Hospitals cannot cope with the demand to help these self-destructing people. What I'm trying to illustrate here is that societies, western, eastern; whatever society there is has a problem, many problems but they are good at not showing it. They control media releases so that the world does not get to know what is really happening in their society. The world is sick Chief, very sick. I strongly believe that mother earth is about to shake itself up and cull many of the human populations. We have produced more than we can consume, we have storage houses filled to the brim with over produced goods that we cannot consume, people are buried in debt, and they have no borrowing capacity as they are over spending their wages. We have destroyed forests and mountains; we have dug up the soil till we found mother earths blood. We have poisoned rivers and are killing ourselves with poisons added to our food, our water. Illness and death are big business; chemical companies control the world by genetically engineering seeds, producing crops that are seasonal, controlling the food source of humanity, spraying chemicals and poisons that get ingested by toddlers. Everything is monetary. It's not about helping one another, it's about taking from the other and that is the sad truth Chief." Ramon stopped for a breath and then continued. "The world is in a very precarious state. Soon they will see firsthand that they can't eat their money, they can only buy so much and in the end there is nothing left for anyone. Only the so called native tribal men will possess the skills to survive and live off the land. Not the younger brother, no not him. The world has seen many saviours, but they refuse to listen to the message they have shared with the world. Every person who has inspired the world to uprise and stand for their rights has been imprisoned or killed and the few above it all remain in control. It is sad that the people, those that have the right principles are always the ones that suffer, the victims. The Mamo in Colombia have been fumigated by the Americans, because they were caught in a drug war. The Americans thought that the Mamo, were the ones producing the drugs imported into the United States and the American president decided that to get rid of their crops they should be fumigated, their land killed, and so they killed many tribes by poisoning. International interference in the political issues of many so called third world countries comes from the United States. They think the world does not see what they do. Little do they know that their land will soon be consumed by mother earth and turned upside down to cleanse the bad blood from the surface of the earth. The little humans that believe they are descendants of the great and powerful will succumb to the power of the great mother. She has had enough and so have the people of the land. For hundreds of years the people of the land have withstood oppression, patiently, at a high cost they endured and suffered the detriment of the white man's invasion. Pillage, rape, plundering and looting; they have taken the children from their families as if they were animals; without conscious thinking of the damage they were doing. The ignorance of the so called great people can be traced back into the distant past. Man never thinks of the repercussions, no! They just become enamoured with their self-aggrandisement and go for it, never considering the consequences of what they do. The world is not a big place any longer. We thought once upon a time that the world was big, so big that we could never make our presence felt. Today we realise that it isn't so. That the little blue rock that spins in the open universe is so small and that we have polluted not only that which sustains us as a human race, but have polluted our thinking, our purpose, and our values as a family of humans. I believe and fight for justice, I believe that we just need a few, a handful of humans to wake up to the call and prepare for what is coming; the ones that will go forward and take the people to the new future and start again. The world is no longer sustainable and it's important that we preserve the ones that will know how to survive, just like Kay-Kay has promised, when the Mapuche gets saved once more from the destruction of Xeg-Xeg they will be home once again." Ramon was entranced in his speech as if he had been borrowed by the mind of a wise being. The chief had tears rolling down his face from the words he spoke. In his heart he felt it, he knew that every word Ramon spoke was true; he himself had seen what was happening in the world and knew that humanity had gone too far.

"Even though my heart sinks with sadness about the truth you speak, I would like to believe that the Gods are listening to our prayers and will intercede by doing or making whatever needs to happen. Happen, so the future of mother earth is safe. I cry because I'm a man that has seen much, has endured much and many times I felt lost without knowing what to do, how to deal with what we were facing. Today inspired by a resurgence of the Mapuche pride I stand strong and even though tears fall from my eyes I believe that we will survive and remain the people that will walk the earth free once again, just as we did long ago. We will be the original people of the land and the Gods will return to talk and commune with us again." said the chief with strength in his voice and tears in his eyes.

Part Ten

Look deep within
Find the loop that entwined the whole
For man's known fault is to leave
An opening or a hole in their thinking protocol.

Ramon asked Jabaro to drive him to town, he needed to communicate with Celeste and see what the others had come up with in the meantime.

Celeste had sent a message with more legal interpretations of native rights. She included a paragraph from the constitutional law of Argentina regarding interpretation of what constitutes being indigenous. It read:

Dear Ramon,

Following my research I have come across the following information which I believe is exactly what we are looking for, we must understand that another definition of indigenous people necessary to understand the following examination of aboriginal social movements in Argentina is that given by the national government.

The Ley Nacional 23302 sobre Política Indígena y Apoyo a las Comunidades Aboriginales (Nacional Law 23302 about Indigenous Politics and the Support of Aboriginal Communities) states the following: Se entenderá como comunidades indígenas a los conjuntos de familias que se reconozcan como tales en hecho de descender de poblaciones que habitaban el territorio nacional en la época de la conquista o colonización e indígenas o indios a los miembros de dicha comunidad.

4 Ley Nacional 23302 sobre Política Indígena y Apoyo a las Comunidades Aborígenes, Article 2.

They shall be considered indigenous communities those groups of families that recognize themselves to be descendants of the populations that inhabited the national territory during the periods of conquest or colonization and indigenous or Indians the members of such said communities). 4

4. National law 23302, about Political Indigenous and support of Native Communities. Article 2.

I think we can use this information together with the previous article regarding indigenous societies described by the U.N. Here we can build a case and send all information to Makkah for the application to the U.N. and the Argentinian government for the recognition of their native rights.

To other news on the front line. I have met a priest through a friend of a friend that is kin in helping out with the Saint Ceferino celebration. He promised to get in touch with the ecclesiastical order and see what he can do about getting all churches to celebrate San Ceferino on the 11th of November 2017.

Things are busy and moving fast, please check the emails from the guys overseas and get moving. There are thousands of signatures already that I'm collating to support our application.

Love you and miss you, always with you.

Celeste, xoxo

Ramon was very happy with Celeste's work. That paragraph would give them the basis for their application and it seemed to fit perfectly. She had stated that she would send all information to Makkah, to prepare an application for the U.N. and the government of the country. Things were moving well, and he could feel the impetus of that movement as a good omen. He responded immediately.

Dear Celeste,

The joy your words brought to me is more than a blessing; I thank you for such great research. Yes please forward all information to Makkah and she will know what to do with it. I shall follow with a message for her to go on and forward applications to the U.N. and government of Argentina. I like the priest's interest and help. Give him my thanks and may we be together once again soon.

Love as always.

R. xoxox

Ramon read emails from many people, however one from Brava brought tears to his eyes.

Dear Papa',

I have great new to share with you; there are many, many indigenous tribes in Peru very interested in joining our march. They have been speaking about a timely reminder to the colonisers of their country about their land, their habitat and their culture. They have realised that they have been exploited for centuries just with tourism alone. They have been used as servants and disregarded from any important decisions in political arenas and the inclusion of their thoughts and what they want. So it's with great pleasure that I stand next to you in this march and may we remind the invaders that we were here first. Stand together and preserve the species, the native people of the Americas. Ecuador, Salvador and Venezuela have also joined us. They have sent word of organising marches in their capital cities and we shall be in touch with them about exact detail.

Love you Papa'

Brava.

PS: Gato sends his love.

Brava was aflame with excitement of being part of such enormous march, a movement that crossed all frontiers and united all the original people of the land. She understood what it meant to fight for ones right to exist. The people of the Americas didn't invade anyone, they were invaded and their right to have a social input in the political decisions of the country was only fair.

Ramon replied immediately to Brava.

My dearest Brava,

I'm so proud of the work you have done, thank you for mobilising the tribes of Peru and neighbouring countries to stand for what is right, their rights to be counted to be included and to say 'No More'. We are making great progress and have found information that will give us a strong stand for law reform and inclusion for the people of the Mapuche nation. I shall forward an email to Celeste who will be in touch with you and all other participant organisers so we have the same important information for the day of the march. I miss Gato also; I shall find a moment to speak to you in spirit soon. Meanwhile take care and keep on fighting for what's right.

Love you more than I can say.

Dad. Xo

Ramon looked through the emails and found one from Saraphina, his daughter in Melbourne. He laughed out loud at reading her words.

Dad! I hope you are doing fine, because I'm in a mood to rip the world apart and start again. Mykah has been lying all along and I have dealt with that, I think he never believed I was capable of such anger. I've had it with men that think they know best. I am now free of his lies. Brava tells me you are campaigning to mobilise the South American countries to stand for their rights. What can I do? Tell me and I'll do it. I can ask my readers to join the campaign as we did with the Colombian Mamo. Brava told me that you want me to wear the tooth necklace so we can speak, I been wearing it since the day she told me. Speak to me soon.

Send me details of what you need me to do to help.

Saraphina.

Ramon knew she was going to be mad at Mykah. She had learned much through the Ayahuasca ceremony about him and came to understand that he had memories about their past lives together all along. Ramon was not surprised to hear she had finished with him; however he was interested in knowing how she finished with him? Perhaps he would speak with her soon to find out.

Anis and Melina had replied, they had added the video of the Mapuche Machi to their web page and wrote an article about the social conditions of the Mapuche people in Argentina. How they were trying to be recognised as an integral part of a society that had forgotten them and how they were standing up for their rights as citizens of the country. They had collected three hundred and forty thousand signatures already from their Dutch website. Links to other partnering websites would only make the number grow. Anis sent a smiley face with the number of signatures, knowing that Ramon would be very happy with that.

David Jacques had linked his webpage to Anis's and had forwarded the short film of the Machi to many organisations that dealt with human rights issues. He was responsible for adding one million signatures to the campaign. Ramon could not believe his eyes. The number of support that people were showing just highlighted one important fact the political front didn't want to acknowledge. People power has an incredible leverage when it comes to bringing a government down or raising people up. The power is always with the people.

Jan from Scotland had added the video to her webpage, the Horticultural society she worked for were great supporters of the Mamo in the last campaign. She had great response from the UK and she had collected thousands of signatures then, her short but friendly email had shown the same support as before, people had loved the short film of the Machi performing her healing ritual and the number of signatures she had collated were standing at two hundred and seventy thousand at the moment she sent the message.

John from Mississippi had moved again amongst the very influential people of great organisations that supported the native rights and titles; he had also collected thousands of signatures and offered advice and support if things got difficult with law interpretations.

Pinky and Alba Luz had joined forces and were getting support from Universities and their students. Activist students had set up a web page that informed the world about many indigenous nations throughout South America. They had included the short film of the Machi and it had raised much attention with three point two million people seeing it; the results again proving to be a great support for the cause.

Makkah had sent an automatic reply saying she was out of office. Ramon sent her a message letting her know that Celeste was forwarding information for her to go ahead and begin paperwork to submit an application to the U.N. Secretary for review of Native titles and Native rights in Argentina. He made it clear that he was in a part of the world that had no electricity and no internet and for her to keep in touch with Celeste and follow the information he would send from time to time. He had to travel for over an hour to the nearest town to access communication and it was difficult to have regular contact.

On the drive back Ramon was quiet for most of the trip; Jabaro asked him if everything was alright? Ramon looked at him with glazed eyes and snapping out of his thoughts smiled and said:

"Jabaro, when you were in Peru amongst my daughter's guests and I saw you, I had no idea what you were bringing me to. What you were asking me to do for your people. Today the world knows about the Mapuche, their situation and what they need. I have received evidence that over four million people have put their names to our application to the U.N. in support of the Mapuche. So really I'm overwhelmed with people's generosity and support... I am amazed that in today's world of small communication devices that grabs people by their ears keeping their heads down that we can reach so many through exactly the same thing that keeps them oblivious about so much. We are winning Jabaro, we are winning!!!" said Ramon with a broad smile.

"I'm glad you came to help us Ramon, you are a man that even though a little unusual, poses a thinking that many are deprived of. But what I enjoy the most about you is that you are such an everyday guy. I'm sure other men with your knowledge would be ostentatious, you know what I mean, high and mighty. But you are a humble man. I've seen you with your family and I see you with the Chief and the Machi and you are always the same. Even when Celeste was here you didn't change, you brought her to everyone's level so that we were all comfortable with each other. Poor and less educated people are highly humble, they treat people of importance with utmost respect, but you remove that from every situation, no one is less than you. I even saw that with Peuchen! I think she finds you interesting!!! She was obviously having trouble making you feel small in her presence, and then again you spoke to her just like you speak to me! That is what I love about you." Jabaro patted Ramon's back as a good friend would.

"Thank you Jabaro, funny you observed that about my behaviour. When I'm facing something powerful, some greater force takes over my entire being. I'm not the one speaking. When I'm talking to any one I'm all ears and feel their innermost sentiment that is what happens. That's all. I am your average man Jabaro, nothing special, nothing at all. However we've got a lot to do ahead of us and things are getting exciting." finished Ramon clapping his hands in excitement.

The chief was happy to see them, they walked onto the veranda and sat down to talk, the cook brought mate and fried cakes. They ate and drank of the green tea as Ramon shared his news. The chief was excited about the new information and could not believe the amount of support the world had shown. His eyes filled with tears of humbleness, people that had never met him or even knew his name had put their name in support of his. Chief Anibal was moved, he felt strong even though he looked vulnerable and his emotions were only of happiness for his people. Perhaps his parents knew something about his future. Perhaps the name Anibal, Hannibal from the original Phoenician language, was the name people of Argentina would remember for ever more. Perhaps he was the chief that would liberate the Mapuche from the oppression of the colonisers into their freedom after five hundred and twenty five years. Ramon spoke for a long time about organising the march, time was moving fast and there were only a few weeks left. Mobilising a whole continent was hard work and he needed to delegate certain responsibilities to others. Ramon asked the chief to organise the Mapuche Araucano people, thousands of them, the more the better he had said to the chief. The Mapuche brothers from across the Andean mountains were to join them sending a delegation to participate in the march and the Mapuche Aymara of Chile were to organise their own march in the capital Santiago. Jabaro was assigned the acquisition of the banners, seven thousand banners with the face of Ceferino Namuncura were to be flying on the march; held by strong Mapuche hands. The Machi was in charge of making sure all traditional costumes were perfectly presented and worn by every person in the march, she herself was to lead the Mapuche women group of dancers and medicine women. Ramon was to spend the next few days in town with Celeste, he was making sure he had access to a computer to keep in touch with everybody involved. He had to follow up on many organised marches all over South America and time was running out. The chief agreed that it was best he was in Buenos Aires and to keep in touch with all others involved and assured Ramon that they were capable of organising their own people and would meet up with him and the rest of the crew on the morning of the 11 of November. Ramon and the Chief spent some time alone after everyone else had retired that night. Ramon wanted to make sure the Chief was clear on the protocol they would follow on the day of the march and that he was comfortable with the speech he was to present outside the Government House at Plaza de Mayo. The chief was ready, he had been waiting for this moment a long time and he was not prepared to miss a minute of such an opportunity.

Later that night Ramon took a walk along the dirt road, he wanted to feel the emptiness of the region and he also wanted to speak to Peuchen. As the stars above, in the dark sky twinkled, Ramon held his medallion and thought of Peuchen. In seconds he heard the whirlwind of her presence. As he looked into the sky, the light that she possessed spun around in a kaleidoscope of lightning and colour, changing constantly until she appeared in front of him as a giant raven, with horse legs, human mouth and eyes.

"Shaman!!! How nice that you have called on me! What can I do for you?" she was happy to see the 'little man' as she fondly called him.

"Peuchen, I have called you to say good bye, I'm leaving this land and returning to the big city. I wanted to let you know that the world will learn about you, and all the creatures of the Mapuche underworld. We have raised awareness in countries that had never heard of your people and they have shown much interest. Stories of the Mapuche will emerge and with it stories of you Peuchen. They will feed life to you so that you may go on and live long into centuries to come, together with your people. It has been a pleasure meeting you and even though I never meant to disempower you by confronting you face to face, I hope that today you understand my need to do so." said Ramon looking at her mixed face of unusual features.

"Shaman!!! You have been such an instrument in the fountain of our life! You have made me laugh!!! Something Peuchen is not known for! And I thank you. Your lack of fear was not an insult to me; it was a test of courage. Humans fear their own demons, and that is what you lacked. You said it Shaman, people feed us with their fears and if they had no fears inside themselves we would not exist. Their demons are what we become! Go Shaman; push that world into a spin and let them know about the Mapuche people, our legends and traditions. But most of all I thank you for the creation of a day for Peuchen. Every year now Peuchen will be ignited with energy and the legend will go on." Peuchen's wings spread over Ramon's shoulder as if the fearsome creature suddenly had emotions.

Ramon retuned to Buenos Aires the next day, this time he took the bus so that Jabaro remained with the chief in case he was needed. Celeste was anticipating his return and could not wait to see him again. There was much to talk about but most of all she wanted to rest in his arms and be held tightly. Ramon arrived in the evening and she collected him from the bus terminal, she ran to his arms and kissed him many times, she was so happy to see him again. Ramon reciprocated the welcome and took her hand as they walked away from the coach. She smiled at him like a teen ager besotted by her first love. Ramon asked a few questions about details regarding the march and the church involvement in it. He said that the Salesian monks were organising their churches and monasteries all over the country to celebrate Ceferino's anniversary. Celeste added that the Catholic Church was involved and there was a meeting organised for Ramon to meet with the Archbishop of Buenos Aires. They were supporting and celebrating Saint Ceferino's tenth anniversary. Ramon felt relaxed, he knew he could count on her; she was good and worked fast, everything seemed to be in order and running like clockwork.

At her apartment, they relaxed on the balcony with a hot drink watching the city traffic go by slowly along the roads beneath them. He asked if she was sure he would not be imposing on her style by staying with her for the next few weeks. Celeste smiled and whispered,

"You can stay forever if you want; there is nothing more fitting than you here. I shall enjoy every minute of your company."

"Gracias Celeste" he said and kissed her gently on the lips.

That night they slept close to each other spooning, breathing gently almost in unison, tired by the long day and anticipation of meeting again. There was plenty of time for love making; now they would have opportunity to go deeper, explore their essence beyond the simple five senses. Ramon wanted to commune with her, to take her to a realm never explored by her. A new level of awareness that dissolved the physical and entwined the spiritual; allowing a connection that they could call on anytime later in life as if they were next to each other.

That night she dreamt of long roads and sunsets, conversation and kisses. Gifts brought to her by his lips, hands and company. He dreamt of spirits, thousands of people and words. His was a meeting in the future, his teachers were showing him what was about to come, the near future. They wanted him to foresee the event, the crowds and the outcome. In the morning they woke up a few seconds apart, she got up and put the kettle on, prepared some croissants and a glass of juice. Ramon watched her from the bed for a moment, taking her beauty in, watching her in her most natural state. He got up and walked to the bathroom to shower, a few minutes later he was back at the kitchen table, holding her, kissing her and assuring her that he loved her. He knew she was feeling insecure because of his lack of interest in making love to her the night before. He whispered in her ear that he felt rested and that she was radiant as the morning sun. Hearing these words she felt better, she let go of any insecurities and hugged him with want. They sat opposite each other and enjoyed breakfast over conversation of the day's plans. They were to meet at three pm with the Archbishop. He was to get in touch with everybody organising the marches in every country and she, Celeste, had a message from Brava about some detail for the march in Peru. Ramon looked over to the desk and saw that she had two laptops set face to face on opposite sides of the desk. A work station for both of them, they would be able to talk and share information as they needed it.

There were many emails from all over the continent; Ramon spent hours replying to each of them, organising and mobilising people in each capitol city. Mexico had introduced him to a ten year old native girl, they had included a short film of one of her speeches, Ramon was in awe of her ability to speak and address a crowd, her eloquence and understanding of the indigenous predicament showed pride and was astonishing. She commanded her words with such strength matched by hand gestures that brought tears to his eyes. In the short film she addressed a group of school teachers on the subject of multiculturalism. In her speech she pointed out the blindness of the politicians to include the many indigenous tribes of Mexico in their multicultural façade. She spoke about her mother teaching her that reading for half an hour a day frees the mind of narrow perceptions and educates the soul. She spoke about being judged and humiliated by others for her native roots, judgement passed without knowing the persons education level and understanding of the bigger picture. She knocked her heart with a closed fist every time she mentioned her heritage and roots. She concluded by saying that if and only 'IF' and when the government of Mexico opened its eyes and saw the richness of the native diversity existing in Mexico today they would be a country that embraced true multiculturalism. When the general populace or leaders of the nation no longer had judgement or discriminating thoughts on cast or creed and allowed these native tribes to be part of the pride of Mexico and included them in political decisions only then will Mexico move ahead. "I get insulted every day for my heritage" she said. "I speak my parent's language because they teach it to me and I am proud of being an indigenous person of Mexico. We are rich in history, traditions and culture. I am proud of my heritage." She finished by thanking the panel for the opportunity to address the people present and mentioning every person on the panel by name and individually thanking them she bowed and left the podium. The crowd present stood in ovation, they had never heard truer words from the mouth of a babe. Mexico had chosen her to speak at the end of their march outside Government House. Ramon agreed that it was a choice that would touch the heart of millions and would give the rest of the indigenous people fuel to stand and be counted.

Many more similar emails, with examples of amazing people from all over Latin America came through, the list of speakers was enormous and strong, leaders of the future, native people who initiated changes in many aspects of society were standing, speaking and telling the world that enough was enough. Brava had included a short video she had filmed with her phone about a man, a native of Peru that had transformed an empty block of land into a diverse extension of the jungle. The land was inherited by him from his parents, who many years back had acquired it and cleared that part of the jungle for the grazing of cattle. When his parents died and he took possession of the land he designed and replanted medicinal plants together with flowers that would attract bees and birds for their pollination and higher canopy plants to shade the lower levels turning a barren piece of land into a paradise. He had been nominated for the Nobel Price twice and had been granted high distinction awards for environmental innovation in Switzerland and in Germany. He was conducting the speech in Lima at the Government House there. Brava was so excited that he had come on board and joined their march as he was well known and of high profile. Thousands were following and joining their march. Ramon spent many more days and hours reading contacting and replying to many more letters. He contacted TV broadcasters and networks inviting them to be present for a multicultural festival of unprecedented magnitude. Not disclosing the real purpose of the march. Celeste contacted the many organisations that supported agricultural development of isolated regions and invited them to attend; she also contacted Native societies and house representatives for native equality groups and smaller minority independent groups, those that were isolated in their campaigns to join the march. Numbers were amounting to thousands and growing by the minute.

Part Eleven

The truth is heard,

behind the words that are said.

Listen carefully

for what it represents.

They arrived outside the Cathedral of Buenos Aires ten minutes before their meeting time. They were ready for conversation with the highest representative of the Catholic Church. Ramon had in mind to appeal to the church for support in the celebration of their only Saint, Saint Ceferino Namuncura. The only Argentinian indigenous Saint proclaimed by the church so far. They were received into the waiting room behind a series of corridors that led from the inside of the cathedral, as they waited Ramon looked at a painting on the wall, a large canvas depicting sacrificial crucifixions and martyrs being penalised for their faith. Eyes looking at the sky pleading to God for mercy. Ramon thought of how religion used the horrific images to make people afraid of committing sins. It was and always had been an indirect way of instilling fear into the hearts of the less educated. They practiced exactly that tactic, punishment in the name of God. Brutally torturing those that refused to accept the European God. They were called in to the next room. The Archbishop was sitting behind an elaborately adorned dark wood desk, gold inlay and rose wood, antiquity common to churches all over the world. The Archbishop was of a kind disposition and invited them to take a seat; he asked for coffee to be brought in and began conversation.

"Ramon and Celeste, is that correct? I believe you have asked for the churches participation on the celebration of the tenth year anniversary of the beatification of Saint Ceferino Namuncura! Am I remembering correctly?" he asked with a soft smile.

"Yes that is correct Monsignor." said Ramon.

"Yes we think that it is a lovely request to make sure the whole of Argentina celebrates their dear Saint Ceferino, we agree that churches in every parish across the country celebrate this day with honour and 'Alegria', 'Happiness' for the native Saint." spoke the Archbishop.

"I'm glad the church agrees to such festivity, we represent the Mapuche, the people of La Pampa, some closely related to Saint Ceferino. We intend to come to Buenos Aires and attend mass in this your church, there will be some Mapuche, a delegation travelling down to Buenos Aires for that day. I would like to ask if you would mind us holding banners with the churches preferred picture of the Saint on it. You know the one? The portrait of Ceferino in his black suit that appears in all the church printed Saintly images." clarified Ramon with the Archbishop.

"No, not a problem at all, we are preparing twenty feet banners that will stand either side of the churches door and invite the faithful to come and celebrate with us. Every church in the country will fly the banners a fortnight before the date." Said the Archbishop.

"Thank you, we appreciate your interest in bringing some healing into many hearts, especially the Mapuche hearts. There are some that think it's a mistake to celebrate and elevate a Mapuche brother to Saintly status but others believe him to be the bridge that unites the modern world with the old. And allows the people to move forward into the future with pride." said Ramon observing the face of the Archbishop.

"Yes, we have invested many years in educating native people in different parts of the country, sometimes we find gems that are the pride of the church and Saint Ceferino is one of them, perhaps the shiniest one of all" the Archbishop smiled again.

"The Mapuche have tried very hard to forget what the church has done to its people, they only ask that they be allowed to celebrate their son, the one offered to the church years ago. They would like to stand proud of their recognised son, the Mapuche known in the catholic religion all over the world." added Ramon.

The Archbishop looked at Ramon in the eyes for a moment; Ramon felt that the man got the meaning of his words. He was not praising the church for beatifying the Mapuche Saint; he was driving a knife into the side of the catholic leader for the destruction they had caused over centuries of indoctrination and control. The Archbishop knowing what Ramon was inferring added that sometimes the work of God doesn't seem fair, but it is he who led us to salvation. He stood up and extended a hand to Ramon and Celeste, saying that he looked forward to seeing them in the Cathedral on the eleventh of November, the special mass would be celebrated at midday. Ramon shook his hand and bowed in respect, Celeste kissed his ring. They turned and walked out the door feeling the eyes of the man in their backs. Celeste asked Ramon why he had not mentioned the march. Ramon replied that they didn't have to know everything, the church and the authorities walk hand in hand, they can block anything they may consider a danger and "I told him that a delegation was coming to Buenos Aires." Ramon smiled a cheeky smile. Celeste smiled back and added "Perhaps you are right, better to surprise them."

That night feeling happy about the progress of the preparations Ramon and Celeste relaxed over dinner, their conversation moved from political issues to personal ones. Celeste wanted Ramon to speak about what plans he had once the march was over. Ramon feeling her need to seek commitment spoke about what the Great Spirit may have in store for him.

"I don't know right now what will happen after the march. I guess I'll find out. Things have a way of presenting themselves and taking me in its whirlwind. But why try to think so far ahead, tonight I want to share with you something very special, very intimate. I want us to commune so that no matter where I am in the world we can always come together as one. Would you be willing to explore a new way of reaching a higher state of consciousness?" he asked looking into her eyes.

Celeste's eyes brightened up her smile broadened with anticipation and in jest she said "I'm into anything that means intimacy with you!"

Ramon smiled and said that it would happen at the right moment. It was true, for an hour later they were naked, facing each other close but not touching, it was only the body heat, their aura that touched them. They looked into each other's eyes for a while, they desired each other's lips and after a while of desiring their bodies Ramon explained to Celeste that she must follow what he said.

"As I breathe out you breathe in, my outbreath is your inhalation, we are not to allow our mouths to touch, just the breath. As you breathe out I shall breathe in, your outbreath is my inhalation, and so on, when I feel the energy lock into a circle of energy between us I shall take you further, all you have to do is trust what's happening and stay in the energy, don't open your eyes."

As they commenced their breathing cycle their bodies pull was stronger, as they closed their eyes, their bodies pulled toward each other. It was hard to keep the distance; their physical energy was so strong that it took conscious thought not to fall into each other. Ramon kept the breathing going, Celeste was feeling faint for a moment and then regained strength, Ramon kept breathing ever so close to her mouth and she found it hard not to immerse herself into his mouth. As the breathing became less conscious she felt that the breath was changing, it became thicker, more solid, more noticeable, real. The energy from their body was now warmer radiating outwards as if each of them was a sun. Their minds became relaxed and filled with light, and as the energy cycled between them, they began sensing a feeling of elevation as if weight was not existent. When Ramon felt they were ready and the connection was deep seated, he touched her index fingers with his causing a short circuit that sent them off their physical body into the ether. In a flash they were out of their body, spiralling upwards in a state of oblivion, entwined in one another. Above them only the consciousness of light, bright white light and no form, they were conscious of the awareness of each other but there was no form, nothing, no shape to be perceived. They spiralled further and as they were engulfed by the whiteness of the light they felt each melt into the other. Becoming one mind, one consciousness, one thought. Celeste could feel Ramon's heart and mind. Ramon could feel her heart and mind. They were one, two halves making the whole. Higher than they had ever been. Complete and whole, in pure form yet without it. They remained entranced in one another for what seemed an eternity, until Ramon gently brought them out of the white light gently into the body, descending, floating like feathers to gently land on the physical self. On awaking from their spiritual union they found themselves entwined in physical form, she was sitting on his loins, he deep inside her and as their bodies came to the realization of this, they orgasmed together in an explosion of light that blanked their minds of their physical limits.

They lay down, melted into each other and drifted into the swirls of colour that had encompassed their awareness. The only reality of their bodies was the knowledge of their hands holding each other; the rest was lost to a technicolour show of light and sound only experienced inside their being.

The following weeks leading to the day of the march were hectic with preparation and communication going back and forth to many parts of South America. Every organised march was getting ready for the day, colourful traditional costumes from every participating tribe or native group were being prepared and beautified; flags, banners, music and dances. Speeches and the participation of thousands of native people standing for their cultural rights. In Argentina, the news had spread through other native groups in the north of the country and they were joining in in the march, they had Aymara roots but suffered the same fate as any nation of pre-Columbian people. Their subjugation and oppression had lasting effects and their denial into society as an equal member was still denied by narrowing their placement in modern society. They also wanted to make a statement of inclusion.

Things in La Pampa were also busy. The Machi had organised for all the women to renew their costumes, colourful dresses and skirts, embroidered and painted shirts, ponchos and head dresses. The men were to wear head bands with symbols of Mapuche origin, white shirts and black pants, ponchos over their clothing of earthy tones woven by the women, designs of Mapuche tradition and history detailing the edges. Banners with the words 'Mapuche Saint, Argentinian Pride', framing the portrait of Saint Ceferino. The Chief had his costume made; he wanted to look imposing with a white shirt and a pair of black pants. Over it a red poncho with black designs on its borders, matching red head band on his head of the same design.

The numbers had reached sixty nine thousand men and women that would be participating in the march. Arrangements had been made for trucks to take loads of Mapuche people to the city and they would travel in the early hours of the morning not to be seen by the towns along the way to Buenos Aires. The least suspicion they raised the better, as it was a matter of surprising the people of Buenos Aires with an invasion of Mapuche people, a parade that infused and filled the streets of the city with colour and music bringing everyone to the streets. TV networks were told that the Mapuche celebration would take place in Plaza de Mayo, outside the Government House at eleven am. They didn't know that the march would start at the Congress house and walk across the city to the Government House five kilometres away giving the cameras a sea of Mapuche colour and banners that went as far as the eye could see. The surprise was to make the headlines, to incite TV networks to show the importance of the Mapuche march, to make a statement and by holding and adding Saint Ceferino banners; they instantly resonated with every Argentinian citizen.

Through the weeks preceding the date of the march, Ramon communed with Brava and Saraphina in a three way conversation that took place in the etheric form. Brava spoke of the arrangements for the march, the increased interest in La Cintura Research Station and the speakers that she had met for the day of the march. Gato was with them and spoke of Atticus development in the ways of jungle. He had learned climbing skills and was turning into a little Tarzan, making it hard to have a restful day with his energetic demands for companionship. Saraphina had explained how she confronted Mykha about his knowledge of their past lives, how he had tried to lie again even though she told him she remembered. "His eyes turned red when I told him about Keeper and the deal with the Goddess of Love. How Cupid was their son, the son he took from her in order to control his memories and possess her for eternity." Ramon was not surprised, perhaps Mykah deserved what he got for keeping secrets from her and making deals with Goddesses that demanded high prices. The girls had been very active mobilising people in Peru and collecting signatures of support for the indigenous people of Latin America. Brava was now well known throughout the neighbouring countries and Saraphina had made the most of her readers support. It was obvious that once again they had started from where they left off, before the Europeans invaded the Americas and put a stop to their work of teaching the people of the land how to live productively in harmony with the earth. Memories of Pachacamac returned to Ramon's mind and the realization that his work was just that, a continuation of something that started centuries ago. When he and the girls had lives in the Inca world, the world that was destroyed by the Spanish and the Church with their lust for gold and power.

Messages came from all over the continent; every city was ready for an early march the next day. They all had agreed that at eleven am their representing speaker would do their speech in front of their respective Governments' House. Ramon's friends in charge of promoting and collecting signatures in support of the Mapuche had reached thirteen million. These would be collated and added to the application to the U.N. and a copy sent to the President of Argentina and Chile. The world had done it once again; they had come together as one people to support the minority groups. The ancient ones, the original people of the land.

Ramon was once again moved by the kindness and involvement of humanity. It was obvious to him that the majority of humanity cared and respected those of a different culture. It was reflective of the hype that had been stirred by politicians in powerful countries, the division of racial groups, the building of walls, the refusals of refugees left to float in the sea to perish. All these had stirred the human heart, cruelty and individualistic ideals had brought the people of the world to stand above representing governments that advocated for differences and segregation of the races. People had had enough; they felt they were not represented by their political figures. Their broken promises and lies had caused much embarrassment and they were feeling disheartened by it. Their support was proof of it.

At seven am on the eleventh day of the eleventh month, the Mapuche began their march. Seventy eight thousand native people marched in straight lines of ten across in perfect unison. The Mapuche led the way with the first sixty nine thousand and the rest was made up of visiting guests from the interior of the country and neighbouring countries from Brazil, Peru, Bolivia, Chile, and Uruguay. They walked slowly, straight and tall, they held their banners flying gently in the morning breeze; drums and other musical instruments filled the air with exotic sounds not heard by many ever before. The Mapuche music had a haunting deep melancholic ring to it, an expression of deep sadness and yet elevated the people's moral to a higher level. The women made patterns from side to side, executing simple steps that created a diamond pattern, their colourful costumes and shiny head dresses chimed as they moved across the street. Minute by minute more and more people joined the parade, within two hours the streets were full of people. Thousands came out of their high-rise apartments to join the celebration some joined the march dancing- sharing the carrying of banners or clapping as the Mapuche passed by. Police were mobilised to the streets, to keep watch over the march; camera crews ran from side to side of the streets in order to get a better angle of the marching Mapuche. Reporters making up words to explain why the Mapuche were marching, they interpreted the banners of Saint Ceferino as a religious march, a celebration of the Mapuche Saint. Every church along the Avenida de Mayo was dressed with banners of the Saint. The Mapuche march was underway, TV networks were televising live across South America. The Mapuche had instigated an international 'stand up for your rights' movement. The tribes of all the countries of Latin America marched on the same day at the same hour in every capital city across both continents. The thousands of people that joined the march where from all kinds of religious and non-religious followings, thousands of Mapuche dressed in traditional costumes walked the streets ten wide in rows that made them seem like a military movement. Banners of San Ceferino blowing in the wind, matching the dance of the flags that swayed on the foot paths and balconies. The churches had long banners the length of their walls, long nylon stretches of material with words that read, The Lily of Patagonia, above the Saint's photograph and San Ceferino Namuncura, his name below.

Arriving at the square, directly in front of the Government House Chief Anibal stopped the March with a sign from his hand. He walked a few paces forward and stood erect looking at the balcony door on the first floor, where the president conducted his public speeches. He took a deep breath and began to talk. All cameras on him. TV and Radio networks trying to capture every word the chief would speak. Live TV showing the face of Chief Anibal on big screens along the Avenida de Mayo for all to see and hear.

"I am Anibal Chipayani, Chief of the Mapuche people. We march here today as a demonstration and in the hope that we let the people of Argentina know who we are. Today we celebrate the tenth anniversary of the day of our Saint. 'A Mapuche Saint.' The only indigenous Saint of South America, where he was beatified in his natal place of birth. The Mapuche Saint is our calling card to the hearts of the Christian people that know, pray and believe in him. As we've learnt he is popular with many and many faithful have claimed that the Mapuche Saint has made favours for them, by healing with his devotion for the faithful." Chief Anibal continued. "I learned from my advisories that the world today, on the 11th of November at 11:00 am celebrates the day of mourning for all those that fell in battle in the Great Wars. It's with that sentiment that I speak to you, with loss; but our loss is the loss experienced over five hundred years of oppression and abuse. We believe that we have paid a high price. The earth that sheltered and gave us all we needed has been stripped of everything. You have been pillaging this land for five hundred and twenty five years and we believe that you have taken enough. We ask for a D day; that the war stops for us as well. Today we have brought a witness to record and accept our submission of a human rights investigation. We claim our space in the land you've invaded; our home. We demand that we be given the lands of the Patagonia. That we be given the freedom to roam the land as we always did. It's our nature. We want inclusion on the business developments and tourism of the region. We want to stand beside your parliament and have our say. "Our vote" with much emotion and strength he concluded.

We call today Mapuche Pride Day, National Pride Day. Our son the Mapuche you adore is the face of Argentina. The world prays to a Mapuche Saint. While his family is pushed around with his people into the dry arid lands against the mountains. Five hundred and twenty five years of resilience and even though we are but a handful left; we stand here today to let the world know that the Mapuche people are still alive and strong!!! Today we dance for you. Today we extend a hand and invite you to join us. Celebrate with us our culture, your culture. The Argentinian culture."

As his words ended Ramon took a step towards the U.N. representative and handed him the paperwork for the investigation of human rights and native titles in Argentina, together with a document that presented results and proof of collated information including fourteen million signatures of support from people all over the world. The U.N. emissary took them in hand as photographers and camera men captured it on film. The drums broke into a rhythm that shook the bodies of all present. The dancers began a dance that turned and chased one another. A simple but contagious celebration of dance. The people started clapping and dancing with them and the streets turned into a festival of colour and music. The TV Networks broadcasting live for the world to see. Every capital city had their leader speak and celebrated equally. The Latin American native people had surprised everyone in the most organised march ever seen in history. It had its effect; it inspired many and brought others to anger. None the less the people of the Americas had amplified the state of affairs in their native communities and countries. The world was witness to their stand. The U.N. was exposed also as a collateral organisation that had played blind to the issues of so many. Five hundred and twenty five years was enough for any race to endure, the world needed to change, to be inclusive of its people and to look out for their diversity. No longer was the human race willing to turn a blind eye to the charade of political lies and profitable arrangements with those in power. The world stood up and made itself counted. The Mapuche stood tall and proud on 'Mapuche Pride Day, National Pride Day' their Saint stood beside them in spirit and in symbolism, a symbolism that unified a nation, the bridge that brought forward change to an ancient people.

The Argentinian Government had no excuse. It had to be responsible for the overlooking of every application ever submitted, a U.N. investigation that would last years had begun. The promise of change, reconciliation and inclusion of the native people of South America had been renewed by an exposure to the world of all the corruption and blind eyes played by authorities that professed equality. South America was claiming back what was theirs. The impact of the marches all over the Latin countries was such that the Northern American brothers joined them and stood for their land rights, stopping, picketing and barricading plans for gas lines, petroleum and drilling of their sacred lands. The earth felt a rise of energy; the human race had elevated their vibration, had overcome borders and embraced their brothers. For a moment every race, no matter what language or culture they belonged to, were one kind united by rights.

The Archbishop looked out the Cathedral door, amazed at seeing thousands of people gathering at Plaza de Mayo. He was never told that the Mapuche contingent was of such capacity. Ramon had tricked him. At that moment the Archbishop recalled Ramon's smile as he said that the Mapuche were trying to heal some old wounds caused by the church. As he listened to the celebrations outside in the square, he saw Chief Anibal and Ramon together with hundreds of Mapuche walk across the street in the direction of the Cathedral. The Archbishop greeted them at the door. Ramon introduced him to Chief Anibal and then both walked in to take a seat in the Cathedral. The Archibishop conducted mass that day, a spontaneous move that required humbleness of heart for the Mapuche were right. All they asked for was their right to be the people they are.

Part Twelve

Deep in the soil of our land
Find the roots of our nation.
For in the leaves that sway in the wind
So dances our seed.

Chief Anibal, the Machi Nora and Jabaro stayed behind to celebrate privately with Ramon and Celeste, they gathered in Celeste's apartment for a glorious range of foods and drinks. Chief Anibal was so happy and emotionally fulfilled that he couldn't speak. He sat silently listening to everyone talking whilst his eyes watched the news showing him speaking in front of Government House. The news feed changed from country to country, showing the uprise of all native nations throughout Latin America. A close up of the ten year old girl addressing the president of Mexico captivated his eyes. Chief Anibal felt proud of the movement he had instigated. At the beginning it started with only one request, to get Ramon to help the Mapuche. At that moment he realized the magnitude of what he had started and how the brothers of South and Central America had been inspired to do the same.

Ramon was listening from his desk; he was reading emails from Brava and Saraphina. Brava had reported their success in the march and how Lima stood by them, there were millions of people that had taken to the streets and joined them. Reports from most capital cities said the same. The world stood by the indigenous nations and showed their support. The Machi, hugged Ramon as he read the emails, she was happy and felt more important than ever, proud to be the Machi of the Mapuche. As Ramon skimmed through the emails that had arrived he spotted one from Lisa, the message line read, "Seeking your help"

Ramon opened the email and read the message from Lisa, stating that she wanted to speak to him about possible help with the Zulu. "There is need to stop the poaching and killing of Leopards, they are near extinction and we need to find a way for the Zulu people to understand the urgency to preserve the species". Please respond urgently. Ramon felt a breath near his ear and with it the words of Don Ignacio, "Are you ready for more adventure"

Ramon knew instantly what was to come, he looked at Celeste who was laughing and talking with the others. He took the scene into his soul and closing the laptop he joined them for a drink and a celebration of a victorious march. The native people of South America will go on, with better laws to protect them and make them part of a society that had pushed them for over five hundred years. Today it marked the end of an era and the beginning of a new integration into the new world.

The end.

Reference:

Indigenous groups view themselves as their own unique nation, but state institutions subsume them to the Argentine nation. In this paper, mention of transnational identification, identities and associations refers to relations between groups who live under different states, as opposed to relations between different ethnic nations. Five of the six largest aboriginal populations in Argentina, according to the Instituto Nacional de Estadística y Censos (National Institute of Census and Statistics), INDEC: the Mapuche, Kolla, Guarani, Toba, and Wichí, all identify with an indigenous denomination that also exists in neighbouring countries, including Chile, Bolivia, Peru, Paraguay and Uruguay.

5 Instituto Nacional de Estadística y Censos, "Primeros resultados de la ECPI: El INDEC ya contó 450.000 indígenas," 6 September 2006. Available from http://www.indec.gov.ar/nuevaweb/cuadros/2/ecpi_generales_13_09_06.pdf 6 See Table 1 for countries in which certain indigenous groups can be found.

Printed in Great Britain
by Amazon

69245269R00069